MOWING FOR JUSTICE

A MERLE MYSTERY

KATHERINE FUOCO FAIRCHILD

PROLOGUE

FRUITVALE, IN FREMONT COUNTY, SITS in the center of a vibrant and lush stretch of the American South. For years, it was as if time stood still in Fruitvale… but in the late 1980s, the community grew and changed. New companies arrived to spur the economy; workers from other states as well as immigrants arrived to work in the new industries and farms and to start small businesses, many family-owned.

The citizens of Fruitvale—except for the suspicious few—received the new residents with welcoming grace.

With a great courthouse as its centerpiece, the village of Fruitvale prospered. Rutted farm roads became paved two lanes; highways expanded and interlaced. That network of interconnected roadways soon required a crew of hardy state workers to mow abundant grass, to hack back the forest overgrowth, to corral the kudzu.

This story is of one of those "heroes of the back roads," a Fruitvale citizen and really good guy named Merle Hucken.

BREAKING NEWS

"Emma Henderson with Channel 10 news, here, alongside Highway 36 in Fremont County.

We've learned a body was discovered by two state highway maintenance workers who were mowing this afternoon. The body was found well off the highway behind a stand of tall pines.

The sheriff's department and agents from the State Bureau of Investigation are on scene.

Sheriff Delbert Judd informs us the identity of the deceased will be announced after a coroner's report and notification of kin.

Again, a body was found out here on Highway 36 very near Marker 45.

More on the six o'clock news."

FOUR DAYS EARLIER...

CHAPTER 1

MERLE HUCKEN PARKED HIS RATTLING pickup on the main drag of Fruitvale Village. Time for a haircut. "Either that or get me a dog collar," he'd told his wife Candy.

At six feet six inches and over 360 pounds, Merle "unfolded" himself from the compact truck's cab. He eased out, head bent forward, one long leg at a time. With hands grasping the sides of the door, he pulled himself to a standing position. Even though his home, a doublewide in Greenview Acres mobile home park, was less than fifteen minutes away, the short ride in the old vehicle was uncomfortable for the big man.

Saturday morning in Fruitvale Village. The summer day was bright and clear and mercifully not as humid as most July days. At the far end of Main Street, the town's distinctive roundabout, the busy hub between the village downtown and the state highway, spun with lighter than usual traffic. At the bull's eye of the roundabout stood the stately Fremont County courthouse, a statue of some-such notable standing sentry to ensure the town kept its historic footing. Mature sweetgum trees provided shade, and lamp posts reminiscent of earlier times alternated along the red brick walkways bordering the wide street.

The air smelled delicious. Cinnamon rolls and sticky buns filled cases in Norma's Bakery. Early's Grill was in full swing with sausage biscuits and hot coffee. And although off Main and a few blocks away—if you were downwind—you could catch the smoky scents of competing barbecue restaurants: Smutts and Son Hickory Barbecue and the newest addition to the community, the Joh Eun Korean Barbecue.

Merle ambled two blocks to Herm's Barber Shop. Fruitvale residents recognized him and called out greetings: "Hey, Merle, good to see ya!" He waved to merchants opening their shops along Main: the old-timey soda shop, the antique store, the used book store, the fancy gift store featuring locally-made pottery.

Affable, congenial Merle Hucken was well known. Volunteer fireman, family man. Kind to all, eager to help, community minded. If you needed anything, call that big guy, Merle Hucken.

He neared the rotating red, blue, and white barber pole of Herm's Barber shop and pushed open the door. Herm offered the best haircuts in Fremont County, along with the latest community news. A sign hung above the mirror: "Tell us some gossip so we can talk about you when you leave."

"Well, if it isn't Merle Hucken, volunteer firefighter who saved Ms. Prater's house t'other day!" Herm called out.

Merle doffed his ball cap. "Hey, Herm, how you doin'?" His forehead was white as cream, the lower part of his face ruddy, slightly sunburned, the result of his outdoor work.

"And heard you saved the old lady's little dog!"

Merle flapped his cap and chuckled. "Found the poor little guy hidin' under some bushes. Scared to death."

Herm shook out a smock and gestured for Merle to sit. Merle sat carefully, the chair hardly accommodating his girth. Herm studied Merle for a moment. "Merle, I'm thinkin' you got yourself a good cook at home with your pretty lady, Candy. Your middle's bigger ever' time I see you."

Merle sighed, patted his belly. "I know, I know. Keep gainin'—gonna do something about it soon. Volunteer firefighter physical's comin' up. Gotta get in shape big time."

Herm flipped the smock around Merle's shoulders. "How's your old buddy Seth doin'?"

"Real good. Workin' together full-time now." Merle shook his head. "Tell you what… all the years knew Seth-er in school, in the army together—now we work alongside. Can't get away from Seth Wilkins!" Merle laughed his characteristic high-pitched "hee-hee-hee."

Herm ran a comb through Merle's chestnut-colored hair. "Yep, you two're joined at the hip." Herm switched to clippers and aimed them at Merle's neck. "You guys still mowing and hacking back? Couple of kudzu fighters?"

"Kudzu fighters! I like that! Yep, just two guys who mow for a livin.' State employees. Pays the bills."

The shop door flew open and in strode Seth Wilkins.

"Well, looky here," Herm exclaimed. "Speak o' the devil."

"Hey, buddy," Merle said. "Wonderin' when you were gonna get the mop trimmed back. Was thinking I might hafta use our heavy-duty mower with the long-arm!" And turning back to face the mirror, he said, "See, Herm, can't get away from ol' Seth Wilkins."

"With you in a minute, Seth." Herm ran the clippers, then clicked them off. "Say, you two, I was out there on Highway 20, and side o' the road was a big ol' recliner chair. Just sittin'. Darndest thing. Musta fell off some truck."

Merle's "hee-hee" escaped. "You'd not believe the stuff Seth and I haul off the road! Mattresses, ladders, buckets, you name it. Recycle what we can, but—sad thing— most ends up in the dump."

And Seth added, "Yeah, we've picked up enough auto parts to build us one funny-looking car, I'm tellin' ya." His face darkened, "Worst part, tho', is picking up dead things. Skunks the worst, for the obvious reason. And anytime there's a pet—dog, cat—even a deer or fox—hard to handle."

Looking thoughtful, Herm held the clippers away for a moment. "You handle it okay, Merle? Ever'body knows you're a big softie."

"Not the best part of the job, I'm here to tell ya."

A dark look crossed Seth's face. "That's for darn sure. Dead things… awful."

Haircuts done, Merle and Seth strolled back to their trucks, passing the imposing building housing the Stags Lodge. "Hey, Merle, didn't your pa belong to this bunch at the Stags?"

"He did. Always claimed they were fine fellows, did a lot of good work for the town. I've thought about joining up one of these days. Hey, I'm getting sausage biscuits from Early's. You want? Come on home and eat breakfast with Candy and me?"

"Thanks, no, Merle. Ma's cooking big breakfast. I'll be in trouble if I don't show up."

"Okay, Seth-er… have a good one. See you Monday."

"Yep… see ya."

Pearl Wilkins shook her pack of Marlboros and tapped out her third cigarette of the morning. She lit the cigarette. Her cheeks drew in; fine lines feathered around her mouth. A chain-smoker since age fifteen, her weathered skin stretched thin, close to the bone.

"I still don't know what the hell you saw in her," she said. Pearl's body, a collection of sharp angles, tensed as she crossed her legs.

Seth dunked dry toast into the runny yolk of his fried egg and shook his head. "Ma, you gonna go there again? Told you it was over and done. Can we just forget it?"

Pearl folded her left arm across her flat midsection and blew smoke sideway. Two fingers of her right hand elevated the cigarette; the elbow rested on the left wrist. "Guess you don't understand how that upset me." She tapped ash into her empty coffee cup and stared at Seth. Her pointed chin tilted down; her eyes drilled him.

Seth pushed away his half-eaten breakfast, wadded the paper napkin, and wiped his mouth. "So, she was black, and you don't like black people. I get that. Whatever you think of her, you missed the part that she was a good person." He tossed the balled-up napkin to the plate.

"Look, son, I told you and told you… we're nice to them, but we don't associate with them. You were raised to know that. Why do you think I sent you to that expensive private school? I'll tell you why: so, you wouldn't have to play sports with them black boys. I did that for you, an' it wasn't easy!"

"And so, I work with black people now, so how'd that work out for you?" Seth stood and pushed the chair to the table. "Leavin' now. Working on the fences out back."

Pearl stubbed out the cigarette. She yelled at Seth's departing back, "I know you got yourself a new girlfriend. She better not be black!"

CHAPTER 2

"**N**OT SO DAMP, TODAY." MERLE Hucken lifted a liter of sweet tea and temporarily rested it on his belly overhang. "Not sweatin' so much. An' it's July, after all."

"Air-tee," Seth replied.

"Say what?"

"Said, it's 'an air-tee.'"

"Honest, Seth, I can't understand a word you say when you got a mouthful of them Lance crackers." He leaned over to look closely. "Those the ones with peanut butter?"

Seth swallowed, cleared his throat, took a swig of his Cocola, swallowed again. "I said, 'it's a rarity.'"

"It's a what?" Merle's ruddy face scrunched up, his eyes—the color of a clear blue sky—narrowed.

"Rarity. Here in the South, a real dry July day… it's a rarity."

"My, you use mighty fine words, sir, to discuss the *weather*."

"You are so ignorant, Merle." Seth replied, pronouncing the word as "ig-nert"… his deliberate device to convey sarcasm.

"Well, thanks a bunch, Mr. Einstein. Guess your fine education made you an expert on *hu-mid-i-ty*? Your low-brow friend here just went to public school." He gulped tea.

"And just in case you've forgotten, Merle, I hated that school Ma made me go to."

"You hated school in general as I recall."

"Cooped up in a classroom, all the rules. Hated that. I'm much happier out here just mowing and trimming, being outside with nobody standing over you. Don't have to think about anything except smooth out that grass, hack back the overgrowth…"

"Me too," Merle said. "Can't even think about workin' in some office. Not for me. Out here away from all's going on elsewhere, there's a kind of freedom, guess you'd say."

Neither spoke for a few minutes. Merle broke the silence. "And to change the subject some, how's your mama these days?"

Suddenly irritated, Seth crushed the cracker wrapper in his fist. "Hateful, sometimes and always. You know how she is…"

"Lemme ask you somethin'." Merle said, growing serious. "Why don't you just move the heck outta your mama's house and get a place of your own? Unless I'm full o' beans, you gotta know you're 29 years old and still living with your mother!"

"Merle, you know the reasons. Ma needs help with the property, all that maintenance, fix the fences… and besides I don't pay rent, so I'm saving a bunch of money to buy a new truck. My ancient Toyota's falling apart. So, I'll put up with her nonsense. For now, anyway."

"How you ever gonna get hitched if you're still living with mama? Aren't girls kinda turned off by that? And 'sides where do you *go?* If you get my drift."

Seth shook his head, took another big drink of Coke.

"And speaking of girlfriends," Merle continued, "what's the story with your 'mystery lady' that no one's met yet. What's she like?"

"Real sweet, nice."

"What she look like?"

"Little. Maybe weighs all of 95 pounds. Tiny waist, but still curvy in the right places. Long, pretty, shiny hair. Soft, soft skin." Seth's eyes turned dreamy; he appeared transported. "She's just beautiful… no other word for it."

"Blonde?"

"No."

"Well, what is it about her? I know your mind's been on somethin' other than work. You nearly drove off into a ditch the other day… you weren't thinking about mowing and trimming!"

"Okay, Merle, you win." Seth's face took a serious turn. "I am nuts about the girl, crazy about her, think about her all time." He took a big swig of Coke. "What else you wanna know?"

"She gotta name?"

"Soo."

"Sue!" Merle chuckled and playfully punched at Seth's shoulder. "Seth-er's got himself a Susie!"

Seth smiled, said nothing, leaned back and closed his eyes for an after-lunch rest.

Merle began laughing. "Seth-er, me and you—how many years now?" He sputtered ice tea. "Went to school with you, joined the army with you, work out here on the road crew with you…"

Seth sat forward and smiled, pushed back his cap. "Lemme think. We were maybe five years old. Kindergarten? Thing I most remember is you'd finish my sandwich, whatever was left in my sack lunch. When I'd get home, Mama'd say, 'What a good boy—you finished all your lunch.' Never had the heart to tell her Merle cleaned it up for me."

Merle laughed his high-pitched, squeaky, infectious "heh-hee-hey."

Seth stuffed a napkin into his lunch bag. "You know, it's me can't get away from you—never thought I'd end up working for the state department of transportation, and who shows up to be my work buddy—nobody but ol' Merle—who stole my choco-late chip cookies when I was in fourth grade."

"I did not steal your chocolate chip cookies. I 'admired' your homemade cookies your mama made so good." Merle's lips formed a sly smile.

"Admired them right down your gullet." Seth brushed crumbs from his sweaty T-shirt. "At least I got a break from you in high school and the couple years we were in the army." He took the last sip of Coke. "Now we're together again—out here mowin' and cleanin' up. Road workers—rain or shine—maintaining the road shoulders. Merle, they oughta call us 'heroes of the back roads.'"

"Got that right. Weren't for us, Seth— the brush'd grow so thick nobody could find the woods and sure as heck nobody could pull a pickup over to the side and park none. And the darned kudzu'd take over, cross to the other side, fence off the road. It's us who keep kudzu from covering the whole state."

Seth nodded in agreement. "Heroes, we are. For darn sure. Saints, maybe."

CHAPTER 3

DOG-TIRED, SETH KICKED OFF HIS grass-stained boots and sat down on the back steps of his mother's house. The day had been long, the earlier dry July weather turning steamy and sticky. He pulled off his damp socks and left them on the step.

"Seth! Supper's on," Pearl, his mother, hollered.

He pulled open the screen door. "I'll wash up. There in a minute."

Pearl set the table and laid out potato salad, fried chicken, sliced tomatoes. Seth pulled out a chair and sat. "Looks good enough to eat, Ma," he said as he filled his plate. "Hot out there today. Thought Merle was about to croak."

"He's way too fat," Pearl announced. "Gonna fall off that mower from a heart attack, one of these days."

"Um," Seth responded, his mouth full.

"Now, son, don't wanna talk about Merle. Who's this girl you seeing? I know you go downtown Fruitvale to see someone. I'm your mama, and I have a right to know."

"Whadya wanna know?" Seth wiped his fingers on a napkin.

"Who are her people? What do they do?"

"Okay, Ma, here's the truth. They're hard-working people. They own a barbecue restaurant, run a business. What else?"

Pearl processed this information and lit a Marlboro.

"Ma, do you have to smoke when I'm eating? You say Merle

eats too much. You smoke way too much. Can't you wait till I'm done?"

Unfazed, Pearl responded, "How long you been seein' her? You're out way late during the week and most all-day Sundays."

Seth set down a drumstick and wiped his fingers. "First met her at the barbecue place—went there with Merle and some of the guys—few months ago." He retrieved the drumstick from the plate, took a bite, and mumbled, "What else you wanna know?"

Pearl tilted her head back and blew smoke to the ceiling. "And what does your 'young lady' do? She work in the barbecue joint?"

"Yes, she helps in the evenings. During the day, she does housework for a lady you probably know."

"And who's that?"

"Maybelle Jordan. Lives over other side of Mossville."

Pearl sprang from the kitchen chair as if she'd been catapulted. "Maybelle Jordan! That witch! How can she work for that terrible woman? She's the worst woman on god's green earth! I won't allow you to see anyone who works for Maybelle Jordan!"

Seth, taken aback, his potato-salad-loaded fork suspended in air, stared at his raging mother. "What… what are you talking about?"

Pearl leaned forward; her non-cigarette hand pounded the kitchen table. "I'll tell you what… that woman's the reason your grandparents divorced. She chased your grandpa, my pa, 'til she finally caught him. She's the reason our family is all broke up! My ma died from a broken heart, 'cuz o' that evil bitch!"

Seth finally found words. "Well… that was a long time ago, and besides my girlfriend has nothing to do with that…"

"Don't matter! That woman's evil. You can't go out with anybody who's workin' for her, and that's final!"

Seth, exhausted from his day in the blazing sun and mowing twenty miles of roadway, stood from the table and walked away.

"Where you going?" his mother yelled.

"Out," he replied.

A furious Pearl Wilkins stood on the porch of Maybelle Jordan's home and pounded the door. The evening light, a palette of summer pastels, still held the sky for a few more moments before sinking behind oak trees in the distance.

Maybelle's post-war bungalow, well-kept and modernized, sported a fresh coat of creamy beige paint. A deep red trim accented doors and windows.

Pearl waited. She glanced back at climbing roses, a bright cheery pink, covering the wire fence surrounding the small garden. Trying to remain calm, she looked up at an enormous Boston fern hanging from the porch ceiling, filling the entire left side of the narrow space.

Rage returned, grabbed at her. She pounded again, hurting her wrist. She shook it to ease the ache. "Maybelle Jordan! I know you're in there! Answer the damn door!"

At last, a face peered through a slatted shutter.

"Maybelle Jordan! I got some words for you. Open up!"

The door opened suddenly. A heavy woman, well into her sixties, held the door open with one hand, the other held a bottle of Bud Lite. "What the hell do you want?"

"Let me in, May, I got something to say!"

Maybelle Jordan, clad in a silk robe, her bottle-tinted ash blonde hair pulled back with a headband, responded, "Say what you need to say, Pearl Wilkins. Seems to me you said all there was to say when you accosted me at your daddy's funeral. Can't believe you have any more miserable things to say that you already haven't said." Maybelle shifted her weight and rested the beer bottle on a wide hip. "You called me names in front of people. You hollered terrible words at me. What in god's name could you have more to say?"

"Let me in, and I'll tell you what I've got to say."

"Say it here, dammit. Get it over with!"

Pearl stepped forward. A big mistake. Maybelle's formidable bulk pushed, nearly knocking Pearl backwards down the steps. She grabbed the porch railing, catching herself.

Pearl's lined, narrow jaw tightened. She spat words through clenched teeth. "Okay, damn you… there's some young thing working for you who's been seeing my Seth. You tell her to get away from my son, or else. And if you let Seth in this house to meet up with her, so help me, Maybelle Jordan, it will be the last thing you'll ever do!"

By now, Maybelle was out of the doorway, on the porch, and hovering over Pearl who clung to the railing. Maybelle leaned her large body forward. "You threatening me, Pearl?" Her overly-made-up face smirked. "And just what are you gonna do, if I don't…"

Pearl dropped down two steps, still grasping the railing for support. She attempted a response. No words came.

Maybelle laughed out loud. "You skinny bitch… you are just pathetic, always have been, sticking your nose in other people's business." Returning to the doorway, she glared down at Pearl cowering on the steps. She swung her arm, grasped the door and slammed it shut.

Pearl, her face drained of color, lost balance for a moment. Her purse fell to the sidewalk, the contents spilling out. As she bent down, the door flew open and Maybelle posed in the doorway. She shouted, "An' maybe you'd just like to know your son's 'young lady' happens to be Kor-eee-an! How's that grab ya, Pearl?"

Shaking and confused, Pearl gathered up cigarettes, wallet, lipstick and staggered unsteadily away leaving Maybelle laughing out loud. "She's Kor-eee-an, Pearl! Your sonny boy's got himself a little Kor-eee-an!"

Seth wanted to be with his girlfriend and away from his furious mother. He headed out to the barbecue joint—even though the object of his affection was not expecting him.

The restaurant, a few blocks off Fruitvale's Main Street, was housed in a squarish, low-profile brick building. Seth pulled his small white Toyota pickup in behind the place. He found a parking spot easily; few cars were there. He'd been there many times—the first time with Merle and their buddies from the road crew. He'd never eaten Korean barbecue before but really liked it. However, kimchi—the fermented cabbage side dish—needed some getting used to.

Kimchi and other Korean specialties were one thing, but Seth had no trouble getting used to Soon Ha Kim, the beautiful Korean woman he'd met there. He'd returned to the restaurant several times with some of the guys and numerous times on his own, just to talk to Soon Ha. With her family hovering around, it took a few visits for him to work up the courage to ask her out on a date. Their first dates were brief and late—after she finished work in the restaurant. After a while, Soon Ha persuaded her mother to allow her to also meet Seth on Sundays when the restaurant was closed. They met at the mall, window shopped, talked and talked, enjoyed a pizza. Before Seth knew it, she was holding his hand and telling him he was the most wonderful man she had ever known. Their dates now ended with tight embraces and long kisses.

The humid evening air heavy and still, Seth stepped out of the truck. As he locked the door, his anger at his mother changed to anticipation of seeing Soon Ha. He inhaled the smoky barbecue smell coming from the building's ventilation system; he felt happier. His keys jingling in his hand, he rounded the building to the restaurant entrance. A neon sign above the door flashed Korean symbols and "Joh Eun BBQ."

Seth eased into the place and craned his neck to see if Soon Ha was in the kitchen. She saw him and flashed her beautiful smile. When she smiled, deep dimples accented her lovely face; and when she smiled, it was hard not to smile back.

Wiping her hands on her apron, she headed straight to Seth. "Set, I so happy you here! Thank you come see me. You hungry? I bring you food, beer?"

"Had supper, Soo, just wanted to see you. How are you?"

"I good. Busy day. You had busy day, Set?"

"Yeah, very hot mowing today."

A woman whom Seth knew to be Soon Ha's mother approached and spoke rapid Korean to Soon Ha. The petite older woman smiled at Seth and gestured to a booth against the wall.

"My mother say we not busy; okay we talk. She say bring you cold drink."

"That's very kind," Seth replied, smiling at Soon Ha's mother. "Some sweet tea would be nice."

As Soon Ha went to get drinks, Seth scanned the restaurant. A bare-bones, start-up with minimal fixtures. Mismatched chairs. Plastic dishes and plastic cutlery. Poor lighting.

Seth could see into the kitchen where two men—whom he knew to be Soon Ha's brothers—worked chopping and prepping meat and vegetables. The two were very involved in their work, not speaking, moving rapidly.

Soon Ha returned with plastic cups of tea and joined Seth in the booth. Her petite frame seemed lost in the deep seat of the booth. A snood-hairnet contraption held back her luminous black hair. "Nice you come here now," she said, looking longingly at Seth. "I so happy when you here, Set."

"And I love it when I find you here," he replied. He blushed, looked down into this drink. "Since the first time I came here with my buddies from the road crew—I like coming back… to see you, to be with you, Soon Ha." He pushed his drink in a circle making rings of moisture on the Formica tabletop. "And the barbecue is great!" he said, altering the romantic moment. "Not like our southern 'cue,' but delicious, tho' I'm still not sure about kimchi… not exactly like our cole slaw." He laughed.

Soon Ha giggled, holding her hand to her lips. "Kimchi have lots garlic, may be too much for you! My mother put hot pepper and horseradish. Maybe some day you learn to like." She giggled again and gazed lovingly at Seth.

Seth fiddled with the paper strip from a straw. "Soon Ha, I'd love to take you out to a movie or supper. Do you ever have a free night? I mean, like earlier, so we could go out earlier on a week night?"

Soon Ha glanced at the kitchen. "I will ask my brothers when is best. They need me help."

"Fair enough. Okay."

"Maybe I call you tomorrow? You give me number?"

Seth's heart leaped. "Yes, call me any time!" He looked into her liquid brown eyes. "Call me *all* the time!" He jotted the number on a damp napkin.

Soon Ha held the napkin with two hands and smiled up at Seth. "I love you, Set. You are kind man. And very handsome to look at."

Seth blushed. "And you are very pretty to look at, Soon Ha, and I, I love you."

CHAPTER 4

Finishing lunch, Merle and Seth sat under the shade of a wide-branching poplar tree.

"So, you wanna mow or you wanna weed-whack with that brand-new string trimmer? Should be workin' real good." Merle jammed the rest of his triple-decker bologna sandwich into his mouth. The heat of the day shimmered; they had ten miles yet to mow and trim.

"Whack, I guess, but let me finish this Co-cola… what you doing this weekend, Merle? Candy feeling better?"

"Some, I guess. She still has the low energy, sleeps a lot. Candy's mom comes to help out with the baby. That woman's a lifesaver. Says what Candy's got is *post-part-a-num* depression."

"That little Madison of yours is sure a pretty baby girl."

"Yep, she's a sweetie. Hey! Maybe you and your Susie'll tie the knot and get you some pretty babies!" Merle's fist pushed Seth's shoulder. "Hey, let's talk about your Susie… you said her folks own a barbecue joint…?"

"Merle, her folks own a Korean barbecue joint. They're— she's—Korean."

Merle's blue-eyes bugged. He stared straight ahead. "Korean? From Korea?" He took a big swallow of tea. "Your Susie's Korean?"

"Soon Ha," Seth said, softly. "Her name is Soon Ha."

Merle stared straight forward. Suddenly he turned his wide

body and looked directly at Seth. "Lemme just say this, Sether. I'm your friend. I'll always be your friend, and if you're in love with a little Korean lady, it's fine by me." His serious face took on a worried look. "But, what about your mama? How's she gonna react when she finds out?"

"She'll throw a fit. Probably throw me outta the house. It's okay. I've already decided to move out if that's what it takes. I want to make a home with Soon Ha."

Suddenly, Merle leaped from his sitting position. "Yellow jacket! Hate those mean son-of-a-guns! Ever time I get stung by one, I swell up!"

"How would you know? You're already swelled twice the size you was when we were just outta the army!" Seth laughed at Merle's agitated efforts to evade the snarling insects.

"This's all your fault, Seth!" Merle yelled as he moved his bulky body away from the flying biters. "Told you we shouldn't gone this side of the road." He ran a short distance, yelling. "Shoulda stayed on the other side by the open area. This time o' year, these woods are hometown for yellow jackets!"

Seth was on his feet. "Get away quick, Merle! There's a bunch more."

Merle hollered and ran a zigzag course. A swarm encircled him. He pawed the air, hustled his 360-plus pounds toward a small clearing and disappeared behind a stand of thick pines. "Git away, you sonovabitches!" His high-pitched voice trailed off…

Seth heard a loud rustling, then a thud. He waited. "You okay, Merle?"

Silence. "Merle? I think the yellow jackets gone now." Seth shoved his hands in the pockets of his jeans and waited. "Merle? You fall down? Where are you?"

A sound ensued, a sound Seth had never heard, never thought his old friend could emit. It was scream-like, but not a scream—

more an animal-wail—the kind Seth never knew Merle held inside. "YYYYYYYEEEEEEEEEE! YYYYYYYEEEEEEEEEE!"

Merle erupted from the stand of trees and hopped from one foot to the other, turning, pointing. "YYYYYYYEEEEEEEEEE!"

"What, Merle, what?"

Merle's beefy body whirled, hopped. He spun, his belly wobbling under his sweaty T-shirt. Dirt, bits of twigs, leaves clung to his clothing. He pointed to the stand of trees. His mouth formed words, but no words came out—only the high-pitched surreal wail: "YYYYYYYEEEEEEEEEE."

"What the hell, Merle…?"

Seth—calm, almost impassive, his hands still buried in his jeans pockets—turned, walked into the clearing—leaving Merle spinning and shrieking. He walked directly behind the stand of pines and looked down to his right at the body of an older woman, dressed in a silk robe. She lay face down, her ashy hair streaked a bloody brown. A portion of her skull was battered in, bone exposed.

She was quite dead. And Seth knew that.

Seth and Merle—waiting, their legs dangling—sat on the tailgate of the flatbed truck loaded with mowers and equipment, a state truck they used every day. They'd pulled the heavy-duty vehicle under the shade of a hickory tree hoping for some relief from the relentless July sun. They slapped away gnats, stayed on guard against another swarm of yellow jackets.

Swarming now were sheriff's deputies, highway patrol officers, agents from the state bureau of investigation, a medical examiner, photographers, Merle and Seth's boss Jorge Cruz from the state highway department, and a few bystanders. "Looky-loos," Seth called them. He counted eleven cars on their side of the road and fourteen cars parked on the other.

They'd been told not to leave, that Sheriff Judd and agents from the SBI would question them. They watched a wave of law enforcement surge back and forth. A few feet away, a woman wearing a jacket emblazoned *SBI*, pointed at tire ruts and dented areas in the grass. A photographer followed closely, his camera clicking.

Seth watched with great interest. "All they're gonna find is our shoe prints and tracks from the mower and the truck, Merle."

Merle held his big arms around his belly, rocked forward, seemed not to hear. "Think I'm gonna be sick." He gagged but nothing came up.

Nearly three hours passed. "Wonder how long we have to wait here," Seth wondered out loud. "You okay, Merle?"

"Kinda sick. Wish the sheriff'd let us leave," he replied, wiping his damp, ruddy face with his cap.

They watched two EMTs produce a gurney. A short while later they re-emerged and placed the gurney, now loaded with a covered body, into the ambulance. A policewoman tied yellow crime tape to a tall scrub pine and walked the tape across to another tree about ten yards away.

"The poor woman," Merle breathed out. "An' I tripped right over her… her just laying there. Wonder if they killed her out here or somewheres else an' then they just dumped her in the woods."

"Dunno… they shoulda just left her where she died… been better," Seth said.

Sheriff Delbert Judd emerged from behind trees and eased his over-fed body under the tape. As he headed to Seth and Merle, a burly man wearing a blue-gray jacket with bold letters SBI accosted him. The sheriff continued walking, the SBI agent dogging him and speaking loudly. "Delbert, this here investigation is an SBI matter. The body's on state property. We have jurisdiction!"

The sheriff stopped in his tracks. "The hell you do! This here's Fremont County, and I'm the sheriff of Fremont County, and I got the jurisdiction!"

The agent scowled, "Telling you, Delbert, we're proceeding with this investigation."

The sheriff replied, "An' I'm proceeding with my investigation, and I'm gonna start by talkin' to the two boys who found the body. An' I'm telling you to get the hell outta my way, Rodney."

The agent threw a dark look at the sheriff but continued walking alongside him toward Merle and Seth. "That remains to be seen, Delbert," he said.

"Looks like you boys came across quite a surprise," the sheriff said as he drew up to Seth and Merle. Perspiring and damp, he pushed his hat back from his forehead and drew a trembling hand through thin graying hair. "Wanna tell me the details? You first, Merle… you the one tripped over the deceased?"

Before Merle could answer, a tall trim woman in her mid-thirties and wearing a chic suit approached. Her long legs drew her up beside the sheriff who, much shorter than she, had to lift up his double chin to look at her. The SBI agent acknowledged her. "Afternoon, Ms. Milwood," he said.

"Afternoon, Agent Taylor, Sheriff Judd. May I listen in? I'd like to make some notes. I was driving back to the courthouse when I saw all the commotion here. Thought I'd stop and see what's what." She flipped open a laptop and steadied it on the bed of the truck.

"If you insist, Ms. Milwood," the sheriff answered. A look on his face conveyed, "I hafta put up with these people."

"Merle Hucken, Seth Wilkins, this here's Tanequa Milwood. She's the new district attorney, will be real involved with this case… I s'pose." It was as if he rolled his eyes at the prospect. "An' this here's Rodney Taylor of the State Bureau of Investigation."

"Gentlemen, what exactly happened this morning?" The district attorney said, taking the lead, her tone of voice all-business, no-nonsense.

Merle, rocking back and forth, his big arms folded across his belly, replied, "Yes, ma'am, we were fixing to get mowing again after lunch when I got chased by some yellow jackets. I ran back there to get away from 'em and fell down over the poor dead woman. Like to be worst thing's ever happened to me." Red-faced and perspiring profusely, he shuddered, looked genuinely ill.

"I thought Merle's having a heart attack when I heard him hollering and screaming," Seth added, an unusual calm in his voice. "I went back there and saw what Merle was yelling about. Poor dead woman there."

"Terrible experience, for sure," the DA said. "Anything you think might be important to our investigation? You see anything seemed really out of place, out of the ordinary."

"With all due respect, Tanequa, a dead body out here off 36's 'out of place'," the sheriff smirked.

The DA smiled, ignored the sheriff's comment. "Let me re-phrase the question. You gentlemen have anything else you might think is a factor in finding the person responsible?"

"Anything you noted that might seem important?" Rodney Taylor added.

Both Merle and Seth thought, shook their heads no. "Do they know yet who the woman is… was?" Seth asked.

"Poor dead woman's Maybelle Jordan," the sheriff breathed out, a catch in his voice. It was as if his guard dropped, his usually arrogant demeanor vanished. He glanced away nervously.

Merle, wide-eyed, asked, "You know who she is?"

Sheriff Judd folded his arms across his belly and hugged himself. His face wore a pained, anguished look.

"Yes, knew her. Many years, knew her." His composure returned, and he cleared his throat. "Now Ms. Milwood here wouldn't know the deceased. She's a brand-new attorney moved here from the big city. Nor Agent Taylor here. They're not so much acquainted with our community," he said.

Unruffled, the DA glanced up from her laptop, "I'm learning the community, but I'm well versed *in the law* regarding *homicide*," she said. She gave the sheriff a pleasant but patronizing smile.

Rodney Taylor's expression looked as if he wished to high-five the district attorney. He said, "The deceased is on state land, so my bureau will have a big role in this investigation. We'll be contacting both you gentlemen soon."

"Well now," the sheriff said, hitching up his trousers, "guess I gotta go notify the next of kin…"

"Who would that be?" Merle asked, still trembling and sweating.

"May didn't have a lot of people. Only one I know of is Alvin Clegg; he's a nephew, I think."

"Alvin Clegg. Didn't we go to school with him, Merle?" Seth asked.

"Right, middle school, then I was in high school with him. Quiet guy."

"Well, gotta get started on this investigation." Sheriff Judd turned to leave. "You boys think of anything important, gimme a call. I might call you and ask more questions later."

"And here's my card," Tanequa Milwood said, handing each a business card. "Please call me,"—she glanced at Sheriff Judd and Agent Taylor— "call *us*, if you have any other thoughts about the case."

"Think we told you all we know…" Seth said. Merle nodded.

As they prepared to depart, Merle handed the keys to Seth. "You drive, buddy, 'case I need to lose my lunch." He settled his big frame into the cab of the truck and held his head.

"Worst thing ever happened to me… that poor woman…"

An emotionally pummeled Merle Hucken drew his battered pickup in behind the doublewide trailer he and Candy and their baby girl called home. He sat for a moment to collect his thoughts; his mind whirled as he reviewed the terrible experience of falling over the body of Maybelle Jordan. He struggled with the fresh memory of finding someone—anyone—*out there*—dead. The day's events grabbed at his heart, his innate sense of justice.

At last, he swung his big body out of the truck and headed to the front door. He sank to the porch steps, removed his shoes and sweaty socks; he took off his ball cap—flapped it a few times. He stood, brushed dirt off his jeans. With spread-out fingers, he shook his sweaty t-shirt, then opened the door.

Candy Hucken, still dressed in her pajamas, held baby Madison. "Hey honey, you're home early," she said. A slight smile came to her lips. On an ordinary day, any small smile on Candy's pretty face cheered Merle. Candy's depression worried him.

Candy's mother, Vivian, a great help since the baby's birth, turned from chopping vegetables on the kitchen's narrow counter. "Hey Merle, you have a good day?"

Merle closed the door softly and stood for a moment. "Not a good day, Viv. May be… one of my… ever worst."

Both women registered surprise. Merle, generally upbeat, the man who found good in all, who always looked on the bright side, wore a look of despair. The anguished turn of his mouth, his staring wide blue eyes alarmed them. "Tell us what happened," Vivian said, looking worried. She set aside the chopping knife and leaned against the kitchen counter.

"Lemme sit down first. Sorry, know I need a shower, but I gotta get through something first." Merle's bulk barely fit on the chair in the narrow kitchen dining area. He placed his elbows on the small table, held fingertips to his temples, took deep breaths. "I… I tripped over a dead body… out there in the woods. A dead woman. I just fell right over her. Worst thing ever happened to me."

"Merle, honey…" Candy stood and handed baby Madison to Vivian who cooed softly, "Come here to Granny Viv, sweet baby Maddy."

"Merle, honey… who…what happened?" Candy, her long auburn hair falling loose over her shoulders, knelt down by Merle and wrapped her arms around his shoulders.

"Seth and I… we called 911… Sheriff Judd, the SBI, the district attorney and a bunch of police people showed up quick. Somebody murdered the poor woman." Merle began to shake and perspire again as he relived the experience.

"Oh, my goodness," Candy whispered, "how awful for you and Seth. Terrible experience. How's Seth doing?"

"He's okay, stayed real calm—surprised me 'cuz he gets real upset when we have to clean up road kill. Yesterday, we cleared a big buck was hit by a truck—middle of the road. Seth went behind a tree and lost his lunch. But today—finding that woman—he was real calm, cool."

Candy leaned her face against Merle and held on to him. She could feel his heart pounding. "It's okay, honey," she said softly.

After a short time, Viv asked, "Do they know who the woman was?"

Merle folded his hands, worked them back and forth.

"Maybelle Jordan. Lives over east somewhere—maybe Mossville. I forget."

"I know Maybelle Jordan!" Viv thought for a moment. "But then everybody kinda knows Maybelle." Moving gently side to side, she held the baby to her shoulder and patted the baby's back.

"Must be," Merle said, "'cuz even the sheriff knew her." He slumped forward stretching his big arms on the table. "Who was she anyway? What was she all about?" Candy rose and began massaging his shoulders. "Was she so bad somebody wanted to murder her? You shoulda seen how her head was bashed in…" He stopped and began shaking again. Candy leaned forward, returned her arms around him.

Vivian, thinking how to answer, spoke slowly. "Maybelle Jordan had lots of men friends." She cleared her throat. "She… uh… *saw* a lot of men. Let's just say, she stole a lot of husbands. It was like men were some kinda trophies—the more she could get, the better she liked it. All men were fair game—young, old, handsome, ugly, single or married—Maybelle would set her cap for 'em."

By now, the baby was sound asleep. Vivian leaned down and placed her on a soft blanket in her playpen and took a chair next to Merle. "Let's just say," she continued, "there'd be lots of wives and girlfriends out there glad she's dead and are thinking, 'she got what was comin' to her.'"

"Mama, really?" Candy asked.

"Yep, Merle, your good buddy Seth's granddad was one of her targets. Seth's mama Pearl and his grandma never forgave her." Viv nodded her head up and down. "Yes, Maybelle caused the Wilkins's to divorce. It was a scandal… one of many when it comes to Maybelle Jordan."

She began to giggle. "Sorry, I know I shouldn't laugh about this… considering poor Maybelle's dead and all, but everyone wondered why Maybelle's house always had such a nice fresh coat of paint now and again and how come her front yard always looked so well-taken care of. Turns out, a painting contractor—who was a frequent "guest" at Maybelle's… was tellin' his wife he had a lot of painting jobs or had power washing jobs over the other side of Mossville. And… a landscape guy took regular care of her garden because she was, you know, 'taking care of him.'" Vivian laughed out loud, then held her hands to her face. "Sorry, I don't mean to speak ill of the dead."

Merle, recovering, said, "So there were lots of people who didn't like her?"

"Ummmm," Vivian replied, "you could maybe say there were some—all men, mind you—who liked her a little *too* much."

Candy began massaging Merle's shoulders again. "So sorry, honey, you went through this today. Musta been so hard, but you and Seth did the right thing—you called the authorities. You did what was necessary. Just sorry it was you who had to find her."

Vivian rose from the table. "Well, you're gonna need you some good supper after a day like today. Let me get cookin' here…"

Candy continued to work Merle's back and shoulders. "You know, Mama, I think I saw Maybelle Jordan a few times. I don't remember her being all that pretty a woman. Kinda big with dyed hair, what Daddy used to call 'horsey-looking'… which, I know, is not nice to say, but she wasn't a real beautiful woman. How'd she get herself all those men?"

Vivian retrieved her chopping knife and slid a hand across the chopping board to push together a pile of vegetables. "Uh, huh. Maybelle was not what you call 'a looker,' not real good looking." She chopped a green bell pepper into quarters then held the knife poised in the air as she contemplated Candy's question.

"How'd she get all those men?" A slight smile crept across Granny Viv's face. "She'd show 'em her titties. That's all it took."

CHAPTER 5

Late that evening, Sheriff Judd arrived at a new apartment complex, a "luxury development," boasting manicured landscaping, an Olympic-sized pool, a fitness center. He approached a concierge desk, showed his identification, and asked to see Alvin Clegg.

The concierge placed a call. "Mr. Clegg says to come on up. Fifteenth floor, sir. Elevator is to the left."

A tanned and fit man in his late twenties answered the door. He was dressed in black jeans, a gray V-neck T-shirt, a silver necklace encircling his neck. A diamond ring on his right hand glinted in light from floor-to-ceiling windows.

"Sheriff Judd! What's the problem?" Alvin Clegg's forehead creased; his eyes narrowed. "Something the matter?"

"Got bad news for you, Al."

"Uh, oh. Maybe you should come inside, Sheriff."

Alvin Clegg held the door open. Sheriff Judd entered a smartly decorated, upscale living area—minimalist furniture with sleek, stainless-steel touches. A contemporary painting, abstract with bold colors, hung above the travertine fireplace.

Sheriff Judd removed his hat and sank down on a chocolate brown leather sofa. "Hard to tell you this, Al. Best way is just to say it. Your aunt Maybelle Jordan was found dead out in the woods off Highway 36. She'd been struck with a blunt object…

her head was… well, you probably don't want to know more than that." He looked up, a glint of tears in his eyes.

Alvin Clegg sat on a leather chair and clutched the narrow steel arms. "Aunt May's dead?"

The sheriff shook his head. Neither man spoke for several minutes. Alvin placed his hands on his forehead and covered his eyes.

The sheriff broke the silence. "You know, I was good friend with May—for many years. I know this is hard, Al. I feel your hurt here, too… you know."

Alvin looked up at the sheriff, "Yes, I'm aware of your relationship with Aunt May."

"You have any idea of anyone who would want your aunt dead?"

Alvin looked down at the designer carpet beneath his feet. He spoke slowly, "I think you know, Sheriff, that Aunt May was the kind of person that either you really liked her or you really didn't like her. I know several people—some married women, mostly—who really didn't like her."

"Probably true, sir. Anyone in particular that you think might dislike her enough to kill her?"

"No one, in particular. Lots of people, in general."

Sheriff Judd shifted forward, his large belly occupying the space between his spread-wide legs. "Al, I hafta ask you these questions: when did you see your aunt last?" He drew a pad from the breast pocket of his shirt.

"I saw her last evening. She'd gone through papers and memorabilia she had from her great-grandfather. Wanted me to prepare them for auction. She wanted my input on the value, whether they were saleable."

"What kinda papers we talking about?" The sheriff rested the pad on his belly and jotted notes.

"From the Civil War. Aunt May's great-grandfather—that

would be my great-great-grandfather—was a Confederate general. Aunt May had all his letters, correspondence with other military—even one from Jefferson Davis—and lots to his wife and family. Actually, Sheriff, I have the boxes in my office. I'll show you…"

Sheriff Judd followed him into a room with black-lacquered office furniture, the desk neat and orderly. A stack of banker's boxes rested in the far corner.

"What we have here," Alvin continued, "are files of the general's correspondence which I have organized according to subject, to whom, from whom… that sort of thing." He pointed to the neat labeling on each box. "And over here," he turned to a credenza behind the desk, "are the other things: buttons from his uniforms, medals, his sword, his belt and holster."

The sheriff seemed surprised. "Never knew May had all this stuff."

"There's one more thing from the collection I can't find."

"What's that?"

"The general's pistol. I know it was with this other stuff; but for some reason, I can't find it. I'd like to go through the house once more if it's okay."

"We're still processing evidence at May's house. Possible she was killed there then the body transported out off Highway 36."

"How do you know that?"

"Some stains on the carpet, that sorta thing. Anybody work at May's regular-like, say a housekeeper, somebody like that?"

"Aunt May had a young Korean girl help her. Said she was a hard worker, said she liked her."

"Know her name?"

"I don't," Alvin folded his arms, thinking, "but Mrs. Edgebert—neighbor across the street—might know. Edna Edgebert—Aunt May said she watched everything, everybody— 'world's nosiest neighbor,' she called her." His demeanor changed suddenly; he slumped to his desk chair. "Aunt May didn't deserve this. My god, I need to make funeral arrangements." He placed his hands, palms down on the desk. "I guess this is beginning to sink in…"

"Real sorry, Alvin. Gonna do whatever it takes to find whoever did this."

"Thanks, Sheriff. Aunt May was one-of-a-kind. Can't believe she's gone." Alvin's gray eyes were tearful as he walked the sheriff to the door. "How's your campaign for re-election going, Sheriff? Did you get my check?"

"Campaign's pretty much on hold, till we find a murderer. Got your contribution, Al. Thanks."

Vehicles and vans from county and state law enforcement crowded the street in front of Maybelle's house. Crime tape encircled the neat bungalow; the once-lush porch fern drooped from lack of water.

The sheriff and the SBI agent stood at the front steps while officers trampled the garden looking for who-knows-what. "Not gonna argue with you, Rodney, I'm leadin' this here investigation. Murder occurred here at the woman's home."

"I'll remind you the body was found on state land, Sheriff," Agent Taylor said. "Therefore, the investigation has to be collaborative… a joint effort." He looked as if he was not prepared to argue this detail further. "We'll share findings. And in that spirit, I will share with you that numerous long dark hairs were found in various parts of the house."

"Young Korean woman worked for the victim. Not surprising there'd be some of her hair 'round."

"You consider her a suspect?"

"Ummm, told she's a tiny thing. Could she have overpowered a woman like Maybelle? Not sure, may be a suspect. What else you got?"

"Grass stains on the carpet. Considerable shoe prints… extend through the kitchen, out the back porch. Blood stains on carpet. No sign of the weapon used to bludgeon the victim."

"Grass stains and footprints?" To control his trembling hands, the sheriff crossed his arms. "Somebody killed Maybelle in her parlor and then transported the body to woods off Highway 36." He uncrossed his arms; they appeared too short for his pear-shaped body. Perspiration rings crept from his armpits. "Well, call me when the coroner's got time of death and all. Meantime, I need to talk to neighbors, see who saw or heard. I'm still leadin' this effort, Rodney."

Agent Taylor closed his laptop and placed it under his arm. "Sheriff, what is it you don't understand about working together to find a murderer?"

The sheriff harrumphed. "I understand real good how to find a murderer, Rodney. So let me do my work."

"Then you understand we share all information between us and also with District Attorney Milwood."

"The DA? You mean that scrawny thing from uptown? Gimme all reports first, and then I'll get 'em to her."

Agent Taylor shook his head in disgust, turned, and walked away.

Sheriff Judd exhaled, extracted his small notebook from his pocket, and headed across the street to the neighbor opposite Maybelle's house.

Before he could ring the doorbell, the door flew open. "I saw it all! 'Bout time you come to talk to me!" Edna Edgebert, her pinched mouth smug and disapproving, held the door wide, "Get in here, Delbert Judd, I got things to tell you!"

"Morning, Edna."

Before the sheriff could remove his cap and enter, Edna Edgebert began speaking rapid-fire. "Seen it all, I tell you! What happened was—I first seen—two nights before—Pearl Wilkins come there and had a knock-down-drag-out with Maybelle—right there on the porch. They had it out, I wanna tell you! Calling each other names and shouting. Heard Pearl yelling at her then Maybelle liked to push Pearl clean down the steps. The next morning, I see the Chinese girl show up for work, then just a few minutes later, she comes running out the door and takes off down the street. 'Bout thirty minutes later, here comes Pearl's son in his little white pickup truck racing round the back of Maybelle's... about ten minutes after that, he drives back out and takes off." Breathless, Edna completed her speech looking as if she'd provided a great service. "And that's the facts, Delbert."

Overwhelmed, Sheriff Delbert Judd shook his head and sighed, "Korean. The girl's Korean."

"Well, they're all the same," Edna snapped. Her pursed lips signaled her continual annoyance with everything. Anything. Life in general.

Delbert looked this way and that, as if attempting to dissect and understand Edna's information. Before he could formulate a question, Edna continued, "An' this must be a real interestin' case for you, Delbert, seein's how you were visiting at Maybelle's at least once a week for how many years now?"

"Edna, you know, you and Maybelle and I all went to school together. We were—uh—friends."

"Friends, my eye, Delbert. You and all the other men went visiting Maybelle—not for friendship. Who you trying to kid, Delbert?"

"I... I..."

"Cat got your tongue, Delbert? Everybody knows what Maybelle had goin' on over there, and you... you... *our fine law enforcement…* was one of her best *friends*! Don't give me your excuses, Delbert! Some of us know the truth!"

Sheriff Judd had had enough from Edna Edgebert. "Edna, you're known as the nosiest woman in the entire region. I s'pose you like your reputation… which you've had since we were kids in school. And since you like to quote 'everybody,' 'everybody' knows your husband Walter Edgebert was one of Maybelle's visitors too! You're just bitter 'cuz you couldn't keep him home!"

"That is none of your business, Delbert! Walter would not associate with the likes of Maybelle Jordan!"

"That's okay, Edna." The sheriff spoke in a patronizing tone. "You believe what you wanna believe…"

Furious, Edna Edgebert yelled, "You, Delbert Judd, are the biggest waste of time! How you got to be sheriff of this county is beyond me. Sure as hell, I won't be voting for you in November!" She slammed the door causing the sheriff to step back, startled.

Recovering, he shouted through the door, "Edna, I'm sending an agent from the state bureau of investigation to take your statement. We're not done with you!"

Edna's voice, muffled, came from behind the door, "Go to hell, Delbert." And she mumbled to herself, "I seen what I seen."

CHAPTER 6

WITHIN THE SPACE OF TWO days, Seth changed—from the cool, calm individual who held it together under difficult circumstances—to a fidgety, nervous man. His smooth, tanned face now carried worry lines, a pinched brow, a downturned mouth.

The change did not go unnoticed by his old friend, Merle—who himself was still experiencing post-traumatic nerves. They needed time—to recover after discovering the gruesome remains of Maybelle Jordan. Jorge, their boss, agreed and gave them a few days off.

Seth, unfocused and agitated, showed up at Merle's home at mid-morning. His usually clean-shaven, angular face showed stubble, his sandy hair slightly better than bed-head. Notorious for starting the day in clean, pressed jeans, he wore clothes he'd worn the day before. Clearly fatigued, he hadn't slept since finding the body.

Merle made a pot of coffee and handed a cup to Seth. He wanted to help Seth—and himself—to put their terrible experience aside and to move on. "Hey, Seth-er, we gotta just get ourselves over this! We're victims ourselves. Innocent by-standers, so to speak. Somebody else's criminal doings affected us. We were in a wrong place, wrong time. We just gotta put it outta our minds. Once we get back to work, out there in the sun and air, we'll be better."

"I know, I know…" Seth breathed out. "I'm worried about

Soon Ha. She worked for the woman, and they might think she…
God, I don't know… I tried calling her at the restaurant—nobody
answers."

"Tell you what, ol' buddy of mine, let's head on over to
downtown Fruitvale and have us some of that real fine barbecue." He gave Seth's shoulder the playful punch. "We'll say hey
to your little sweetie, Susie."

"Merle, told you, her name is Soon Ha."

"I know, but Susie's easier name for me. You can introduce
us! She'll be real impressed when she sees you hang out with
me." Merle laughed his high-pitched "heh-hee-hey," the first time
he'd laughed in days, though he was working at being cheerful.

Seth gave a weak smile. "Okay, you'll like her… when you
see how sweet and pretty she is…"

"Wait till she gets a load of *me*… *better* worry she doesn't
throw you over when she sees what a hunk I am!"

"Cut the crap, Merle. We'll take my pickup, if you can fit in
it."

The two friends headed out and arrived at the restaurant just
before the lunch crowd. As they entered the restaurant, Seth
looked for Soon Ha. He glanced around and saw her mother talking to a patron. When she saw Seth, she appeared frightened and
literally ran, disappeared into the kitchen.

"Let's just take a seat," Merle suggested. "Maybe your
Susie's back in the back somewhere."

They sat at a small table near the window. Shortly, Soon Ha's
mother came out of the kitchen with an armload of plates and
placed them in front of other diners. She turned quickly, but Seth
stood in her way. "Where's Soon Ha?" he asked.

"She not here."

"Where is she?"

Glancing around nervously, Soon Ha's mother said, "She go
back. Korea."

"She's gone? Korea? Why?"

"She have go back." Soon Ha's mother tried to get around Seth who stepped sideways to block her exit. "I busy now. You go away," she said.

"I want to talk to her brothers."

"They busy. No talk now. You go away."

Seth stepped aside and let her pass. He looked into the kitchen at Soon Ha's brothers. They scowled as if threatening, daring him to question further. His exhaustion took over. He turned and said to Merle, "Let's go."

Merle raised his big body from the small table. "Somethin's not right here, Seth-er. I don't feel good about any of this."

CHAPTER 7

A WEEK LATER, SETH AND MERLE returned to work mowing, trimming, reporting road damage to their boss. They didn't converse much. Each harbored unsettling thoughts about that awful day on Highway 36.

In the afternoon, a tropical storm whipped in from the coast; the weather turned threatening. Storm clouds rolled in dumping rain in on-and-off intervals. Lightening popped in the sky. When a bolt came much too close, they decided—for safety—to knock off for the day.

Seth pulled in at his mother's house to find the sheriff's car and another police vehicle parked at the front door.

Seth was exhausted—this was all he needed—to have to go over the whole bad scene again, the finding of Maybelle Jordan out there in the woods. Since the discovery, he had not slept, had no appetite, his usual calm replaced with agitation and worry. His once steady nerves were frayed, his quiet demeanor shattered. He stepped out of the pickup to hear Pearl shouting, "Dammit to hell, Delbert, you know we did not have anything to do with Maybelle! My son is a good boy. He could never hurt anyone!"

Seth stopped at the front door. His mother's voice was clear as a bell. "My Seth just got mixed up with the Korean bitch that worked for Maybelle. She's the one that's killed her!"

Seth's heart fell to this stomach. For a moment, he considered fleeing, running away, getting lost from all this drama. Instead, he did his best to reclaim calm nerves. He opened the screen door and spoke firmly. "Sheriff, neither my ma or I had anything to do with this."

The sheriff pushed back his hat. "Don't think so, Seth. You're under arrest for the murder of Maybelle Jordan."

A sheriff's deputy, a young lanky man, observed but said nothing. He pulled handcuffs from his belt. He held them out as if ready to spring.

Pearl yelled, "Delbert! You sonovabitch. You! Delbert! You were carrying on with the witch for years and years. She was the only woman you could get 'cuz no other woman would crawl in the sack with you! And now you come here and arrest my son? What kind of low-brow sonovabitch are you?"

"Now, Ma," Seth said, drawing up every ounce of calm he could muster. "I'm sure there is some mistake. Sheriff, I had nothing to do with this. I know the Korean girl who worked for Ms. Jordan, but that's all. I never went there…"

The sheriff, his rounded face red, his double chin trembling, replied, "That so. Well, we got us an eyewitness account of you there early on the morning of July 16."

"Eyewitness?"

"Ms. Edna Edgebert, neighbor who lives directly across from Ms. Jordan, saw a small white pickup, older model—just like yours—go in behind the house. Then she saw you in the vehicle pulling away and leaving."

"She's wrong. Why would I kill Maybelle Jordan? I didn't even know her."

"Ms. Edgebert also witnessed your mother here, Pearl Wilkins, threatening and arguing with Maybelle late on the evening of July 14. And, we have further evidence she was there—a cigarette lighter with the initials PJW—laying in the grass near the steps to Maybelle's house. PJW—stands for Pearl Jean Wilkins, if I'm not mistaken."

By now, Pearl had caved into a heap on the sofa. "I went there to tell her off, but I… I did not kill her." Her low-octave smoker's voice croaked, "She yelled at me, pushed me down the steps. I dropped my purse, my lighter musta fell out… but I didn't kill that bitch, and neither did Seth!"

Seth spoke, slowly enunciating every syllable, "Sheriff, I did not kill Maybelle Jordan, and that's the god's-honest truth."

"That so, Seth? How do you explain further evidence: your size ten shoe prints on Maybelle's parlor rug, her kitchen, an' her back porch? Prints that just happen to match the same boots you left out there on your mama's back step?"

Pearl sprang to her feet. "Shoe prints? What kinda goddam shoe prints?"

The sheriff straightened his rounded shoulders, reached to his waist, and hitched up his trousers. "Ones with lots of grass stuck to 'em, stained right good with the good green color of grass. And who here makes his livin' out there mowin' grass?" The sheriff looked very self-satisfied, as if he's just completed an Oscar-worthy performance.

The sheriff continued, "So what we have here is your son getting revenge against the woman who hooked up with your pa, Pearl. Everybody knows 'bout that. You two worked together to get rid of Maybelle. And we have time of death, right at the time Seth here showed up at the house." Sheriff Judd turned his deputy. "Hank, cuff this man here." He turned to Pearl. "Pearl, not gonna arrest you right now. You'll be charged later as an accessory to murder. Don't even think about leaving town."

Pearl, her head down on the sofa, moaned, "You son-of-a-bitch, Delbert. We did not do this."

Seth, shocked and confused, could not comprehend. "But I…"

"No more buts, Seth Wilkins. You're under arrest. You have rights to a lawyer. Not jailing your ma so she can arrange for y'all's representation."

The deputy yanked Seth's arms behind him and snapped on the cuffs. Seth felt as if he had left the real world and was floating in a crazy nightmare. The deputy led him to the police cruiser, pushed his head down, and snarled, "Get in…"

The backseat of the cruiser was narrow; Seth's legs cramped up. He shuffled his lean body to sit sideways.

Worse than the discomfort of the handcuffs and the cramped police car was his worry about Soon Ha. He had no idea where she was, what was going to happen to her.

Near tears, his heart thudding and aching, he thought, "How did it all come to this?"

CHAPTER 8

Lᴇᴛʜᴀʀɢɪᴄ, ᴅɪsʜᴇᴠᴇʟᴇᴅ, ᴡᴇᴀʀɪɴɢ ᴀ ꜰᴀᴅᴇᴅ robe, Candy Hucken stepped out on to the porch of the doublewide to collect the morning paper. She wanted to be in bed, to sleep, to not face the day, but the baby needed to be nursed. She forced herself to care for her baby even though it gave her no joy at all. She asked herself over and over again, "Why do I feel like this? I'm married to a good and wonderful man, I have a beautiful and healthy baby girl, a devoted mother who helps enormously." She didn't understand, could not shake the sadness, the lack of energy. It was if dark clouds enclosed her, preventing her from stepping into the sunshine.

Candy reached down to pick up the paper. She slipped the plastic from the rolled newspaper and held it open. "Oh, goodness," she said out loud. She returned inside; Merle was finishing breakfast, baby Madison propped up in her highchair. Merle took a bite of oatmeal then made a funny face at the baby.

"Merle, this is some bad news." Candy placed the paper on the table. "They arrested Seth." She sank into a chair and pushed hair from her face.

Merle put down the spoon and read the headline aloud, mumbling through a mouthful of oatmeal, "Seth Wilkins Arrested for Murder of Maybelle Jordan."

Merle, his blue eyes wide and incredulous, swallowed. "No!

I've known Seth all my life. He could never do such a thing. This is all just wrong…"

Candy glanced through the article. "Remember what Mama said about Seth's granddad, that Maybelle Jordan broke up their family." She looked up from the paper and shook her head. "Seth's not a vengeful kinda guy—wouldn't, couldn't do something like this…"

Merle pushed his oatmeal away. "Your mom said Maybelle caused a lot of ill will, but with Seth's family—that was years and years ago, sounds like." He read on. "Uh oh, says they have hard evidence that Seth Wilkins was at the scene of the crime."

"Merle, how can this be?"

"It can't be," Merle said. "It just can't be." He tightened his fists and held them to the table. "There's gotta be more to this story. I know Seth's innocent."

Candy thought for a moment. "We know Pearl hated Maybelle. Could she have done it, and Seth's taking the blame?"

Merle shook his head. "I dunno—I can't believe Pearl, even, would do this. I tell ya, Candy, I got some questions."

"Do you think they'll let Seth out on bail? Maybe not, for murder."

"I dunno that either." Merle stood and tapped his finger to the table. "This is just wrong. I'm gonna ask some questions." He pushed his chair to the table. "And I'm gonna start by having a long talk with my old buddy, Seth. He's got some explaining to do… how he got himself in this mess."

"You going to the jail and talk with him?"

"Yes, I am. But first, I'm gonna tell a pretty lady how much I love her and this here pretty baby, too." He leaned over and kissed Candy. "You feeling better, sweetie? Anything I can do for you?"

Candy burst into tears. "Merle, I don't deserve you," she sobbed. "I wish I could just… I could just…"

Merle leaned down and held her close. "It's okay, sweetie.

This is gonna pass. You'll get better. One day at a time. I'm here for you."

His heart aching, he had to put up a good front for Candy, and now for Seth as well.

At the Fremont County jail, Merle pulled his pickup into visitor parking and strode into the vintage red brick building. He approached a deputy sitting behind a desk.

"I'd like to see someone held here. His name is Seth Wilkins."

"You family?" the deputy snapped.

"No, sir, but we're friends since age five—school together, army, work together."

"Only family allowed."

"We are kinda family—like I said…"

The deputy tipped his head up and down, scrutinizing Merle's wide and tall stature. "You look familiar," he said. "You volunteer fireman?"

"Yes, sir, Seth too—both of us…"

"You fight a fire— 'bout a year ago—on Shelby Lane?"

"Yes, sir," Merle said, thinking, "elderly lady, maybe?"

"That lady was my granny! She's grateful to you guys for savin' her place. You guys did a great job!" The deputy rose from the desk, reached into a drawer, and handed Merle a visitor pass. "Wait in that room over there. Visitors there."

Merle attached the pass to his shirt pocket and waited for Seth.

"I didn't kill her!" Seth paced the jail's small meeting space. A deputy stood outside the open doorway of the overly air-conditioned, badly-lit room.

Merle sat at a metal table; his hands folded. "Let's start at the beginning. How'd you get yourself mixed up in this?

"Long story."

"I got long ears. Try me."

Seth continued to pace. Merle was losing patience. "Seth, did Soon Ha kill her?"

"No! She couldn't. She wouldn't. She said the woman was nice to her. Paid her well. No *reason* to kill her—besides Soon's so small, she couldn't knock out somebody big."

"Wouldya just sit down, Seth? Let's talk this out." Seth sagged to a hard chair.

Merle waited for Seth to focus. "Lemme ask you this: if she's innocent, why'd she run away?"

"She'd be deported if the police came. No green card, not a citizen."

"How do you know that?"

"She told me. She was not here legally. Her visitor's visa had run out."

Merle looked directly into Seth's sad eyes. "Did she go back to Korea? Any chance she can renew that visa and come back? She could testify you didn't kill the woman… maybe." Merle was thinking hard, trying to find a solution to Seth's nutty dilemma.

"I dunno. Korea, maybe L.A."

"L.A.? Los Angeles? Why L.A.?"

"There's a big Korea town there. She's got cousins there."

"Was she deported—or she just left? Ran away to California?"

"Merle, I dunno. All I know is we were happy and talking marriage and now this. Why am I in here? How'd I get myself in this mess? I'll tell you: I just fell in love with Soon Ha Kim, that's all!" Seth began to cry; he leaned forward and placed his head on folded arms and wept.

Merle was at a loss for words. All he could do was pat his old friend on the shoulder. "Yeah, love does things to you…"

Seth lifted his head; tears rolled down his face. "Ma will tell you I fell in love with the wrong kind—one of them *slanty-eyes*." Seth choked out the words. "That's what she called my Soon Ha. Hurt me so bad, Merle." He sobbed. "Don't know how much of this I can take. I've lost Soon Ha, my mother hates anyone I love, I'm in jail… accused of something I did not do!" He slapped his hand to the table.

"Looky here, Seth Wilkins, you gotta help me, help you," Merle said quietly. He found a tissue in his shirt pocket and handed it to Seth. He gave Seth a moment, then said, "Answer me some questions: do you know when Soon Ha was last at Maybelle's house? When did she last clean up there?"

Seth wiped his eyes, blew his nose. He swallowed hard. "Day before, probably. She always went real early in the day—sometimes, she said, Maybelle wasn't even outta bed. She'd go in and do the laundry and clean the kitchen, make her coffee. She told me then she'd help Maybelle box up a lot of papers and stuff."

"Papers and stuff. What kinda stuff?"

"Soon called it "old stuff and paper from old war." When I asked was it from the Vietnam war, she shook her head. When I said from World War II, she said no, and when I said a war older than that, she said yes. I finally decided it was the Civil War, because she said there was a sword and an old pistol and some other things. And lotsa papers."

"Why was Maybelle going through all this stuff?"

"She didn't really know, but Maybelle's kin was coming to get it and do something with it."

"Kin? That would Alvin Clegg. Right?" *I need me a talk with Al Clegg.*

Merle returned home to find Candy, still in pajamas, holding baby Maddy who had just finished nursing. "Did you see Seth?"

As he washed his hands in order to hold the baby, Merle related details of their conversation. "Now I got more questions than ever," he said. He bent his tall frame forward and lifted the sleepy baby from Candy's arms. He rocked her gently, smiled at the baby's contentment.

He returned to thoughts of Seth. "Seth's innocent. I know he is. You know somebody pretty darn good when you grow up with him, work with him. I mean, we're out there mowing, then we take a break, an' we talk about everything… how much he cares about his mom but how she just makes him crazy with her racist stuff. How nutty he is over Soon Ha, the first girl he really, truly loved. And I probably couldn't know anybody better— 'cept maybe you, sweetie. I mean—during tick season—after Seth and me are done mowin', we check each other for ticks. You know somebody pretty darn good when you pull a tick outta a buddy's butt."

His wide brow furled; he looked at Candy with questions. "How do I find a way to save my good friend from going to prison for something I know he didn't do?"

"You have questions. Go to people who have answers," Candy suggested. "Why don't you talk to Alvin Clegg? Maybe he has some insights." She rose quickly from the sofa. Merle watched as she showed more energy than usual and settled at her computer. She Googled Alvin Clegg.

She peered at the computer screen. "He co-owns that antique shop and art gallery 'cross town. Here's his number." She jotted the number on a slip of paper. "Call him. Ask him about Seth's girlfriend, if he knew her, that sorta thing…"

Merle's smile and intense blue eyes said thank you without speaking.

I so hope this means Candy's snapping outta this depression-thing.

On Saturday morning, Merle settled in at a table at Hardee's. Through the window, he watched Alvin Clegg exit his shiny BMW and walk to the entrance. He wore linen Bermuda shorts, a T-shirt, too-classy sandals for a Saturday morning at a fast-food place. He wore a gold bracelet and the large diamond ring.

Merle stood and extended his hand. "Thanks for coming to meet me, Al. I just wanted to say how sorry I am about your Aunt Maybelle. It was me, you know, with my buddy Seth who found her that day."

"Yes, I know, Merle. Good to see you." Alvin Clegg took a seat opposite. He folded his hands on the table and looked directly at Merle. "Glad to have this opportunity to have a conversation with you, Merle. Always wanted to tell you how I remembered you from school. You were one of the few kids in school who was really nice to me. When we were growing up, I was shy, introverted, got bullied a lot—but you were always nice to me, kind to everyone, so I'm glad I have this chance to tell you that."

Merle was taken aback. "Gosh, Al, never knew that." He smiled and said, "I do remember a time we had with that kid… what's-his-name… Justin-something."

Alvin chuckled. "Yeah, you sent him packing when he pushed me around on the playground. You saved me from a real boxing match. Thanks."

"Ah, kid thought he was tough stuff, and I was just a lot bigger. No big deal." Merle stirred two sugars into his coffee. "Candy and her mom, Viv, and I wanted to give our condolences about your aunt." Merle looked down at his coffee. "Terrible way to die. Candy says I'm haunted by finding her—like that—out in the brush." Neither man spoke.

"Appreciate that, Merle." Alvin stood. "Let me get a cup of coffee. Back in a second."

As he watched Alvin Clegg order a large latte, Merle organized his thoughts and listed questions in his head. When Alvin returned to the table, Merle said, "Another reason I wanted to talk with you, Al… my good friend Seth Wilkins is sitting in the county jail charged with murdering your aunt. Sheriff Judd says he and his ma were taking revenge against your aunt. I know Seth's innocent. What's your take on things?"

"Well, Aunt May had her enemies, you know. She hustled other ladies' men—won't make excuses for her. But, at the same time, she was generous, donated to causes, wasn't stingy with money. She paid my college tuition, most of it." Alvin blew steam from the top of his latte. "Oh, there were times when I was embarrassed to be related to her, but I think most people have one or two relatives they're embarrassed by…"

"Got that right," Merle chuckled. "Jailbird cousin of mine, sent up at least three times. Next time, don't think they'll let 'im out!" He swirled his coffee and looked into the cup. "Lemme ask you this: when they ask you who could have done this terrible thing, what do you say?"

"It could be anyone… any one of the women Maybelle ticked off, a guy she told to leave her alone. Merle, I really haven't any idea."

"What about the Korean girl worked for your aunt? You know Seth was nuts about her, was dating her. What do you know about her? Could she have killed your aunt?"

"I've thought about that, Merle. I really don't think so. Aunt May liked her a lot, relied on her, said she was a hard worker, understood what needed to be done, didn't have to supervise her much. Even trusted her to help box some important papers Aunt May collected."

"Papers?"

"Our family's related to a Civil War general. Aunt May had a huge collection of his memorabilia. I was helping with it. We were going to put it up for auction. I have most of it—at home—all ready to go."

"Most?"

"Missing an important piece, a pistol—was in pristine condition—never fired. Very ornate, all documented. Now, I can't find it. Nowhere to be found."

"Whadya think happened to it?"

"No idea. Maybe the Korean girl stole it; maybe she thought she could sell it. Don't know."

Merle was still in a quandary. *Got me more questions than answers. What do I do now? Talk to more people about this? Can't shake this feeling something's just not right, not making any sense.*

CHAPTER 9

A T THE END OF A long day mowing along the soggy, muddy shoulders off a back road and having to pull a cranky mower over for numerous repairs, Merle decided to drop in on Pearl Wilkins before heading home to Candy and Maddy.

He parked his big body on Pearl's front porch and pulled off muddy shoes. Standing in his damp socks, he removed his cap and rang the bell.

Pearl, cigarette in hand, appeared. "Hey Merle, come on in," she said. Her whiskey-and-cigarette voice was subdued. "Could use some company."

"Hey, Ms. Wilkins, wanted to see how you're doing, see if there's any news from Seth's lawyer. That public defender any good?"

"Lousy. Overworked. She's got hardly no time to meet with Seth and me and figure the case out. She says she'll get back to me, then I don't hear from her. I call and call. Nothin'." Pearl took a long drag on the cigarette, the ash drifting on to her lap. She brushed her jeans frantically, her motions reflecting her agitation. "The girl's so damn young I don't think she's even got a license to lawyer. Where do they find these children and call 'em 'attorneys'?"

"So, no charges have been filed yet? Thought that had to be done in order to hold somebody in jail."

"I dunno. That stupid-ass Delbert Judd's calling the shots."

She stuffed the nub of the cigarette into an over-full ashtray. "Idiot arrests my son. Makes up the whole thing about revenge bein' why…" She held up two fingers as quotation marks. ". . . *we did it*. I sure as hell didn't like Maybelle, but the last thing I'd do is hit her over the head with something." She lit another cigarette.

"Tell you what, Ms. Wilkins. I'll go and have me a conversation with Sheriff Judd. I got some questions."

For the first time in days, Pearl's pinched, angry expression softened. "You do that, Merle, an' come back and tell me what's what. I sure would appreciate knowing."

"I s'pose you asked for this meeting, Merle, 'cuz you got some more real evidence for me, some additional information?"

Sheriff Delbert Judd, with his rotund body and ruddy jowls, did his best to look professional and important. "We got solid evidence that your buddy Seth Wilkins killed Maybelle Jordan then he dumped the body—placed it where he *knew* y'all would find it—when you were out there mowin' and all. Make it look like he was innocent—since he's got you as part of the alibi. Plain and simple." He hitched his pants. "We got motive; we got evidence. Crime of passion, out of revenge. That's the sum total." He gave Merle his best smug smile. "So, whadya got to say further?"

Before Merle could continue, the sheriff blustered, "And you *knew* Seth was up to no good, didn't ya?"

Merle responded, "You know, Sheriff Judd, I grew up with Seth, I work ever' day with him. I know him. He did not kill that lady. He may have been seen at the woman's house, but that was because his girlfriend worked there. Maybe he just went there to see her before he headed on out to work. There's maybe some explanation; but he had no reason to, did not, kill the woman."

"You're way off base, Merle. He went there to satisfy his mama's hate, do in the woman who took up with his granddaddy. Or maybe he had another reason—maybe he thought he could take up with May—an' she told him to get lost, maybe she told him she was too old for him. I dunno… but we got his shoe prints and an eyewitness. That's good enough for a court of law."

"And what kinda weapon you think Seth used to kill Ms. Jordan? Where's your blunt object you say did her in?"

The sheriff gave his smirking smile. "Oh, you some kind of *de-tec-tive* now, Merle? Some kinda good ol' boy Columbo? You an *in-vest-i-ga-tor*?"

Merle smiled and spoke slowly. "Now sir, I know I'm just a 'good ol' boy' who mows for a livin,' but I know right from wrong—and my good friend, Seth Wilkins, is in jail for something he did not do." He folded his arms across his wide chest. "You're right, I'm no detective; but I gotta believe there's more to this than it looks like on the surface."

The sheriff stepped back, as if his guard were down. "Best not get involved here, Merle. Let us trained professionals deal with this."

"I can't help but be involved, sir, 'cuz if you recall, I'm the one who tripped over the deceased lady. And it's my best friend you're accusing here, so I'm involved—even if I'm just a guy who mows grass out there…"

Merle's words yanked at the sheriff's arrogant composure. Pearls of sweat formed on his balding head. "I caution you, Merle, once again, let us professionals take care of this case. Now I gotta get back to work. Goodbye, Merle."

"Yes sir, I gotta get back to work too." He turned to leave then rotated his big frame to once again face the sheriff.

"Lemme ask you one more question, Sheriff… Alvin Clegg

tells me there's a valuable Civil War pistol missing from his Aunt Maybelle's collection. Could that have been your murder weapon, and if so, where is it?"

"Well, there you go! Seth went there to steal it; probably thought he could sell it for a pretty price!" The sheriff perspired heavily now; sweat rings advanced.

"And along that line, lemme ask another question… Seth's in jail, doesn't have the pistol—so where is that pistol?"

"Dammit, Merle. You ask too many goddam questions! You best watch your step, boy!"

Without answering, Merle turned and left. *Sheriff doesn't have all the facts that's for sure. Wants an easy slam-dunk conviction, but doesn't wanna do the work to find the facts.*

CHAPTER 10

The next evening, after another long day, Merle returned home weary and aching. Granny Viv was preparing supper, baby Maddy was propped up in her highchair, and Candy—wearing her faded robe—sat at her computer.

"Hey, Viv," Merle said as he entered. He smiled at the baby and cooed, "How's daddy's girl?"

Viv turned to greet him. "How you doing, Merle?"

"Back's killin' me. Yeah, I know, I know, it's this big belly that's pulling me over, hard to stand up straight. One of these days, I'll lose some weight."

"Nobody said anything about your belly, honey. Sorry your back hurts. Hazard of the profession maybe?" Candy asked.

He leaned over to kiss Candy, "I'll be okay. Whatcha doin', sweetie?"

"Oh, lotsa things. Looked at photos of old Civil War guns—like the kind you said Alvin said went missing. Learning stuff about Korean culture, that sorta thing—nothing in particular. And looking at how murder's prosecuted under state law. How was your day, honey?"

"Wow, not as interesting as yours! Mine was just long, hot, full of gnats… but all good," Merle laughed. "Lemme shower, get cleaned up for that good-smelling supper Viv's cooking up."

Later, they sat down to meatloaf, mashed potatoes, green beans. "Any news about Seth and the charges?" Viv asked.

"Seth's mom tells me there's all kinds of delay, the public defender isn't even talking with them. I dunno—it all worries me. I told the sheriff how I know Seth's not guilty, and he accused me of bein' a wanna-be detective. When I asked him if he knew yet what kinda weapon was used, he acted all nervous. Something goin' on with that guy."

"Oh, I'm not so sure," Viv said as she squirted ketchup on her plate. "Delbert's just incompetent. Everybody knows it… surprising he was ever elected sheriff. I even wondered if the last election was 'fixed.' Now he's up again this November, and we'll probably have another four years of his bumblin' around."

Candy pushed a chunk of meatloaf around her plate. "I was thinking, honey. Why don't you go over to the Korean barbecue place and just look around again? Who knows, maybe the Korean girl has sneaked back home, or someone there might tell where she is. I don't know, but just get a feel for what's what. Might not lead to any answers, but might be worth a try."

Viv added, "That might be good, Merle. Tomorrow's Saturday, go on over there and have a lunch, scope it out."

Merle thought for a moment. "I could. Not sure what I'd find out." He shoved a forkful of food into his mouth. "But," he mumbled, "there's an old saying my granddaddy used to say, 'If you don't show, you'll never know.'"

The next day Merle put on clean jeans and pressed shirt, readied to head to the Korean restaurant. "Why don't you come with me, sweetie? We'll have some Korean 'cue and some of their cole slaw—what they call kimchi."

Candy held the baby; she wore her uniform of the past months: her plaid pajamas. "I'll need to nurse Madison, don't think I can be gone that long." She detected Merle's disappointment. "But you go ahead, honey. Thought I'd call Granny Viv, maybe she and I'll put Maddy in her new stroller and take a walk in the mall."

Merle's heart leapt. This would be Candy's first interest in getting dressed and going out. "I think Granny Viv and Madison Hucken would like that!" He grabbed his cap. "We'll talk 'bout our 'adventures' this evening." He kissed her goodbye. "I love you, pretty lady," he said as he closed the door.

Merle found parking behind the restaurant and entered through a side door. It gave him a good view of the men working in the kitchen. Soon Ha's brothers: Lean, fit men—about the same age as he, Merle guessed. He'd never noticed their arms before. Muscled with sleeve-like tattoos. Two serpents—Merle wasn't sure if they were snakes or dragons, maybe alligators—intertwined on each man's left arm. Their right arms carried a series of stars—different sizes—extending from elbow to wrist. Thinking about the "serious tats," he glanced around for a table. He chose the small one by the window where he and Seth had sat briefly on the earlier visit.

Soon Ha's mother watched Merle from the kitchen. She spoke to another woman as if to say, "You go wait on that man." The woman approached with a menu. "Hello, what you want drink?" she asked.

"Sweet tea, if you got it," Merle said. She spun away.

Another man, woman, and a boy Merle guessed to be about ten years old took seats at the table to Merle's right. Merle turned to them. "Say, you know Korean food? I like the barbecue, but I'm not up on these other dishes. Anything you've had here you liked."

"Sure. If you like the barbecued pork, you'll probably like the *buldak*—a spicy chicken. One of my favorites. How do you feel about kimchi?" the woman replied, as she stowed her handbag under the table.

"Oh, I like it. One time I had it here—was with some of my work buddies—it was so spicy—made us all sweat!"

The man laughed. "It'll do that to you! If you're up for the risk, I suggest the kimchi fried rice, *kimchi bokumbop.*"

"Thanks, that's what I'll order." The server brought tea and took Merle's order and the other diners' as well. When she departed, Merle said to the family, "Heard you speak Korean to that lady. How'd you learn the language? You really know about the food."

"We lived in Korea for many years. Expats. I worked for an American company—lived in Seoul for five years, then Busan for four years, and finally Daegu for six years."

"We really like the culture, the people, the food," the woman added.

"Wow, sounds like you had some real good experience there. We here have lots to learn about places like Korea, but we share our church with some Korean Baptists. We've gotten to know the family of our Korean dry-cleaners—where I take my good black jeans to be cleaned once a year."

Merle's dining companions laughed out loud. "Yeah, Koreans start small businesses, work hard, do well in the U.S."

"I heard there's big town of Korean people in Los Angeles now."

"Oh yes, Koreatown Los Angeles is a big enclave. Many thriving businesses there, and unfortunately some criminal business too," the man said.

"Whadya mean?"

"Ever heard of the Kkangpae?"

"Gang-who?"

"Heard of the Yakuza?"

Merle shook his head.

"You heard of the Sicilian mafia?"

"Oh yeah, the *I-talians*," Merle said. "Like the Sopranos. Heard of them."

"Well, the Kkangpae are the Korean mafia. Like the Yakuza in Japan, or the Sicilian mafia."

"Lemme think now. The mafia here—they run drugs, prostitution, that sorta thing. Same thing with the *grangpay*?" The expat couple smiled at Merle's mangled effort to pronounce the word.

"Pretty much," the man responded. "Same criminal activity. They're very brutal guys—some say more so than the Sicilian or Japanese mafia."

Their food arrived. Merle surveyed the plate. "Hey, this looks good. Thanks for putting me on to this." Merle spread a napkin on his big belly. "Lemme ask you another question. The two cooks there in the kitchen. What's with their tattoos? That have special meaning in Korea?"

The man looked down at his plate then took a sip of iced tea. "I'm sure it's not the case with these guys here, but those tattoos in Korea indicate "thug" or "street tough." Maybe when they were growing up there, they had to join a gang just to survive. Now that they're here with a legitimate business, doesn't mean a whole lot."

"Sir, ma'am, everything you told me is so interesting. I'm gonna stop asking you questions so you can eat this good food. I've really enjoyed talkin' with you."

"Same here. Say, here's my card," the man said. "I'm an adjunct professor at the university, also do some business consulting. If you know of someone who wants to do business in Korea, or has questions about visiting Korea, anything, have 'em call me."

Merle examined the card. "Thanks, Mr. Evans."

"Dave, call me Dave. And this is my wife Karina, and this is our son Michael."

"And *Mashikeh-mogo,*" Karina said.

"Whadya say?"

The couple laughed again. "It's like 'bon appétit' in French—'enjoy these good eats'!"

"Same to you, Dave, Karina, Michael. Thanks! Oh, sorry to trouble again, but lemme ask one more question. If somebody was not supposed to be here, say like illegal, how hard would it be to hide out in that Koreatown in L.A.?"

"Not hard. Probably could stay anonymous there. For a while, anyway." Dave Evans replied.

"Real interesting." Merle shoveled a forkful of fried rice into his mouth. "Um, this is gooooood."

Merle arrived home to find Candy snipping tags off a frilly baby dress for Maddy. Candy was dressed in neat jeans. A nursing mom, she wore a loose bright-blue top over her fuller figure. "Look, Merle, isn't this the cutest?" she said, holding up the baby dress. "Maddy's gonna look so sweet in this! Granny Viv and I had fun looking at pretty girl-baby things. How 'bout you, honey? How'd it go?"

Without speaking, Merle gazed at his wife, his first-ever-and-only girlfriend, the love of his life.

"Honey, everything okay?" Candy asked. She tipped her head, questioning. Her freshly-shampooed hair gleamed in the sun from the window.

"You look sooooo pretty," Merle breathed. "You just look so fine, my pretty lady." He leaned forward and kissed her. He was so happy to see her dressed and happy about something. He leaned back and sighed. "To answer your question, I learned some about Korean food, that a little Korean lady could get lost in Koreatown in L.A., that there are some really scary dudes called the…" He glanced at David Evans's business card and the letters his lunch-companion had jotted on the back. "It's spelled K-k-a-n-g-p-a-e. Korean mafia, tough bunch. Maybe you could Google it for me sometime."

"Sure, honey, I can do that," Candy said.

"Where'd I put my good black jeans? Think I'll take 'em to our trusty dry cleaner, Jimmy Chung—whether they need cleanin' or not."

CHAPTER 11

MERLE PARKED IN FRONT OF Rite-Clean Dry Cleaning & Wash and Fold. He grabbed his black jeans, hauled his body out of the pickup, and entered the establishment. "Hey there, Jimmy," he called to the man at the counter.

Jimmy Chung, a lean man with a quick, agile body, smiled broadly, his face showing pleasure at seeing Merle. "Merle Hucken! How ya' doin'? How's Candy? How's that beautiful baby girl of yours?"

"Good, sir. Candy's feeling better, and the baby's doin' great."

"Marie was saying the other day, she'd missed seeing Candy out and about, that she was gonna call and say hey. Don't know if she did or not… but know what, our churches have their joint pig pickin' coming up a week from Sunday. Y'all gonna be there?"

"Ohmygosh, totally forgot about it. With Seth being charged and in jail…"

Jimmy Chung's genial expression changed. "Kills me Seth's in jail. Known Seth forever. He'd never hurt anyone."

Merle shook his head. "You know it, Jimmy… only person who doesn't know it is the sheriff. But I'm trying to get him, maybe the DA, to review the facts. Seth's gotta be proven innocent, 'cuz he is."

Jimmy looked thoughtful. "The 'truth will out,'" he said.

"But hey, back to the pig pickin.' You and Candy gonna be there?"

"We never miss a Korean Baptist Church doin' alongside the Regular-ol' Baptist Church doin'!" Merle laughed his high-pitched giggle, then added, "If Candy's not up to going, her mom Vivian will join me."

Jimmy flashed a look of understanding. "You know, Marie kinda went through that after our junior was born. I'll tell Marie that Candy's still having a hard time. I know she'll make an effort to talk with her."

"That's real kind, Jimmy, I know Candy'd perk up to hear from Marie. Say, is Mr. Smutts, the pitmaster, gonna do the cookin' again this year?"

"As always, bringin' the big ol' cooker, loaded with pork, as always."

"Always lotsa fun," Merle added. "We Baptists can put on a good spread—hush puppies, slaw, Brunswick stew, banana pudding. Umm, huh, can hardly wait!"

Jimmy Chung laughed out loud then turned to Merle's black jeans lying on the counter. "Hey, didn't we just clean these six months ago? They need cleaning again so soon?"

"Jimmy Chung, I know you're pullin' my leg. I just need to look spiffy—just keeping my slick-looking jeans lookin' spiffy."

Jimmy Chung guffawed as he wrote the ticket. "When you need these, Merle—for that reception President Obama invited you and Candy to?"

Merle chuckled. "Next week's fine. You know, Jimmy, if you weren't a dry cleaner, you'd be a great comedian. You got a given Korean name? Could be your stage name."

"Oh yeah, I was born in a village south of Seoul. My parents named me Joonsuh Chung, but I was six when we came here, so in school it was much easier to be 'Jimmy Chung!' More accepted, it's good ol' Fruitvale, after all."

Merle thought for a moment to phrase a question about the Korean barbecue place, maybe Soon Ha's family. He turned, about to leave, then asked, "Speaking of good food, Jimmy, your family still cook Korean-style food?"

"When Marie's not fixin' spaghetti and meatballs."

Merle leaned his head back and emitted his high-pitched laugh. "An' speaking of food, you ever eaten at the Korean barbecue, Joh Eun Barbecue, I think it's called?"

Jimmy Chung's amiable expression turned dark. "Nah, you ever seen the guys in the back? Ones with the tattoos? They make me nervous… my pop says they'd be gang guys back in Korea." He handed the ticket to Merle. "But they do cook good. Some people rave about the food."

"The barbecue is good," Merle said thoughtfully. "Well, always good seein' you, Jimmy. See you week from Sunday for some good Baptist-cooked 'cue. And I'll get my jeans when I pass by again."

"We'll get those jeans all snazzy for your big event at the White House, Merle."

Laughing, Merle gave a fake salute and departed.

For certain Jimmy Chung doesn't think much of the Korean barbecue guys. Wonder what all that means…"

CHAPTER 12

T HE SUNDAY EVENING WARM AND pleasant, the sunset emerging in shades of rose and blue gray, Merle and Granny Viv arrived on the sweeping lawn behind the Fruitvale Redeemer Baptist Church. The annual "supper on the grounds" was getting underway. Merle carried a large box lined with parchment paper and holding six dozen warm biscuits; Viv had spent most of the day mixing, cutting, baking for the event. She carried a box holding three jars of her homemade peach jam and a giant jar of honey topped by another box with six-dozen brownies.

The aroma wafting from the pitmaster's cooker scented the area and set a congenial ambiance for the joint event of the two Baptist churches, the Korean Baptists and the "Regular Ol' Baptists," as Merle described his church. Long planks covered in lengths of crisp white butcher paper, balanced on oil drums, some on sawhorses—served as tables.

Jimmy Chung and his father were unfolding chairs and setting them at the tables.

Merle called out, "Hey, Jimmy. Hey, Mr. Chung!"

"Candy not with you?" Jimmy asked.

"Not up to it," Viv answered sadly. Jimmy Chung pointed across the lawn. "Marie's over there, looking forward to seeing you, Miss Vivian." Viv nodded and smiled.

Merle and Viv made their way toward the serving tables, greeting old friends along the way.

The pitmaster, Mr. Gabriel Smutts, the tried-and-true local expert on local style barbecue, tended the cooker. He wore bibbed blue denim overalls, the straps held by shiny brass buckles at his shoulders and at his chest. A checkered kerchief circled his broad neck; a bright-red ball cap covered his steel-gray hair. He lifted the cooker lid and poked at grilling meat. The cooker, a converted oil-drum-type contraption welded to a frame on wheels, was hitched to Mr. Smutts's 4X4 pickup truck. As he lifted the cooker lid, tantalizing smoky smells wafted out and over the crowd.

Members of the two churches arrived with arms loaded—tubs of coleslaw, hush puppies, baked beans, Brunswick stew. Huge pans of banana pudding, along with plates of cookies, brownies, coconut cakes filled an entire table. Another groaned with gallons of sweet tea, air pots of hot coffee, and ice-filled tubs packed with canned soft drinks.

Merle set the box of biscuits on the table and strode up to the pitmaster. "Hey, how you doin,' Mr. Smutts! See you got your extra-fancy cooker out today."

"Yes, sir, Merle, only the best for this fine crowd—this 'pig-rig' holds 'lotsa pig—'nuff for a crowd this size." The expression and tone of the congenial gentleman changed. "They gonna let Seth outta that there jail? He ain't no killer."

"Mr. Smutts, you know that, and I know that, just that Sheriff Judd doesn't know that. Been worried about Seth, his mom says he's not eating much, gettin' skinny…"

Mr. Smutts set down his barbecue tools and huge oven mitt, placed his big hands on his hips. "When we's done here, I'm gonna take Seth a plate. I know Jeffrey, the jailer, and he'll let me slip it in there for Seth."

"Mr. Smutts, you are a gentleman and a kind man. Maybe your good cookin'll cheer him up some, put some meat back on his bones."

Mr. Smutts glanced past Merle, and his genial face changed expressions once again.

"Evenin,' Sheriff."

The sheriff pushed past Merle to grab Mr. Smutts's hand and pump it hard. "Nobody cooks better than you, Gabriel," he exuded. "Only the best from the cooker of Smutts and company."

Mr. Smutts extracted his hand from the sheriff's grip. "Thanks, Delbert, know you enjoy a plate of 'cue now and again."

"Sure do, Gabe, an' here's some of my pamphlets about the up-comin' election, 'an I'd sure appreciate your handin' these out in your community. I'm workin' for the people here."

Mr. Smutts found a stack of "Vote for Delbert Judd" pamphlets jammed into his hand. He looked down at the paper with a startled look. "Um, huh," he uttered. The sheriff flew off into another direction glad-handing his way across the lawn.

A mischievous look crossing his wide face, Mr. Smutts whispered to Merle, "Lemme distribute the sheriff's prop-a-gand-a…" He tossed the sheaf of pamphlets into a trash bin behind the cooker. He gave Merle a knowing look and a broad smile.

Merle and Pitmaster Smutts, both big men with arms folded, watched as Sheriff Judd worked the crowd, picking up babies, tickling toddlers under their chins. Mr. Smutts turned back to his cooker, "Two-faced, son-of-a-gun," he muttered under his breath then whispered to Merle, "Watch him, Merle, he's got litty-bitty bottles of Jack D., those airline kinda ones, slips hooch into his sweet tea. I don't know who the fool's foolin'… by the time, this here pickin's over, he'll be staggerin' and slobberin'…"

"Mr. Smutts, if I didn't know you better, I'd take it you hold Sheriff Delbert Judd in low regard," Merle said, trying to smother his "hee-hey" giggle.'

"Tellin' you, Merle, if'n Seth was an African-American boy,

Sheriff Judd have 'im sent up to Central Prison by now, with no chance o' gittin' out. Tellin' you, Merle."

Merle's heart sank as he thought of his best friend ending up in a prison for "worst offenders." He shook his head and said, "Can't even think 'bout that, Mr. Smutts… I'll let you get back to your cooking."

"Good to see ya, Merle," Mr. Smutts said as he lifted the cooker lid and checked on the roasting pork. "I'll be passin' by the jailhouse and seein' Seth gets a big ol' plate of good eats."

Merle joined Viv to continue their rounds of greetings and "how you doin's." Merle worked the crowd in his own way. Head and shoulders above others, folks gravitated to him. "Hey, Merle, how you doin'?"— "tell us how Seth's doin'."— "how's Candy and the baby?" Merle spoke to everyone, thanked all for their concern for Candy, gave a full report on Seth—emphasizing, over and over, his innocence.

"Suppertime!" Mr. Smutts called out, "Time to eat! But blessing first!"

Members of the two churches circled the laden tables and Pitmaster Smutt's cooker for the blessing of the food. All bowed heads, as the Very Reverend Cho and Reverend Jedforth stepped forward. Reverend Cho began, intoning in Korean, and ending with "Amen." Reverend Jedforth continued, his booming baritone voice rising and falling, "Lord, we're asking in two languages today to bless this food and for your blessings on this assembly of good people. Thank you, Lord, for the hands who prepared this delicious meal, and thank you for the hands that brought this to our table. We thank you, oh Lord, for the fellowship we share today—with our neighbors and friends. Amen." A chorus of "Amen" followed.

"Come an' git it," Mr. Smutts hollered. A line quickly formed as the crowd grabbed plates, and Mr. Smutts loaded each with the savory meat.

Good-natured arguments arose concerning the proper sauce for the barbecued meat. "Stay true to 'cue—the southeastern sauce," one man argued. "Vinegary, peppery. None o' that sticky sweet, Texas-style."

"Hey, don't mess with Texas," another shouted. Laughter all around.

Merle, under Candy's orders and Granny Viv's gaze, spooned smaller amounts than usual, trying hard not to overindulge. Viv glanced approvingly at his plate. "Good for you, Merle," she said.

"I'm trying, Granny Viv," Merle said, feigning his sad-sack look, "but what am I gonna do when I get to that dessert table? I could wipe out pans o' that banana pudding, all by myself."

"Think about staying healthy, and all that. All good things in moderation."

"Yes, ma'am, I'm trying…"

Merle and Viv, with their plates of slaw and sides and Mr. Smutt's perfectly-roasted pork, found that Jimmy and Marie Chung and their family had saved seats for them at their table. Merle settled between Jimmy and his father while Viv sat next to Marie.

"Wanted to tell you, Miss Vivian," Marie said as she buttered one of Viv's lightly-browned, light-as-air biscuits. "I so understand what Candy's going through. Went through something similar."

"Tell me about it," Viv said, her kindly face registering interest.

"When Junior was born, my mother came from South Korea, stayed a month with us, I was so happy… had my mom here, a healthy baby… everything's great." Marie placed the buttered biscuit on her plate. "Then it was time for her to leave. The moment she was on the plane and departing, I started weeping, couldn't stop. All I could think was "I can't do this without her help, I can't take care of a baby all by myself." She lifted a fork and stirred it into coleslaw. "But Jimmy was so good to me, helped so much. He found a really good counselor who put me with a support group of other women. Took time, but I got through it and understand myself a lot better."

Viv listened, nodded. "Candy says she knows how lucky she is, what a good husband she has, what a beautiful healthy baby girl she has. She tells me all the time she appreciates my help. So even she doesn't understand why she feels so sad, so unable to get interested in life." Viv dabbed her mouth with a napkin. "I just don't know… she still doesn't want to face the world, get dressed, go out…"

"I'm going to come visiting, Miss Vivian, have me a good talk with Candy, see if I can help some."

"You do that, Marie, anytime… please… so appreciate if you do that."

Merle and Jimmy Chung's father discussed Seth's situation, the facts of his case. The conversation moved to the up-coming election and who was worthy of their votes. Jimmy lightened the discussion by saying to his father, "Pop, Merle brought his good jeans in last week. For the six-month cleaning. Candy and him have a date at the White House for a fancy reception."

Mr. Chung laughed out loud. "But Mrs. Candy and Mrs. Vivian bring their "go to church" in more regular! Even when they don't get invitation to White House!"

The group chatted on into late evening. "When's our annual Korea Night?" Viv asked Mr. Chung.

"December 17," Jimmy's father answered. "We cook big Korean food then right before Christmas holiday," Mr. Chung replied. "Many special Korean food."

"Looks like we got ourselves a new Korean barbecue place here in Fruitvale," Merle added. "Think they'll show up for the feast on Korea Night?"

At first, neither Mr. Chung nor Jimmy responded. At last, Jimmy said, "New business. Yeah, maybe. We'll see how they do…"

"I always look forward to Korea Night," Viv said. "Wonderful food and fellowship as always." She looked at her watch, "My, getting late, time flies when you're having fun."

The crowd gathered up containers and took down the make-shift tables, stacked chairs, and cleaned up the grounds. Mr. Smutts closed up the cooker, shook hands, and received praise from the entire crowd for his fine cooking. He received a round of applause as he pulled away in his big pickup and the cooker floating on behind. He waved and smiled, "See y'all next time!"

Vivian and Merle helped with the final cleanup, said goodbye to many friends. "What a wonderful event," Viv said as they got into Merle's pickup. "I so wish Candy'd felt up to coming. She would have enjoyed seeing Marie and the Chung family and all the nice people here today."

"Me, too," Merle responded. "Wish Seth woulda been here too. Visiting him tomorrow."

CHAPTER 13

FLUORESCENT LIGHTS ACCENTED THE GRIM starkness of the jail's "inmate meeting room." Merle pulled back a chair, took a seat at the cold metal table, and waited.

Soon Seth—escorted by a sheriff's deputy—stood at the open door. He wore orange coveralls, his sandy hair slicked back, his demeanor that of a beaten-down man with ten days of jail time weighing on him.

Merle stood to greet his friend. "Let's talk, Seth-er. How you doin'?"

Seth pulled out the chair across from Merle and slouched sideways in it, his elbow on the table. "I feel like it's the end of my days, Merle. I've messed up so bad, it can never be fixed right again."

Merle sat, leaned in, tried to make eye contact. "Why?"

"I dunno. Don't feel hopeful at all, that I'll ever get outta this thing okay, that I'll be proved innocent. That I'll be ever be with Soon Ha…" His eyes welled up. "My life is over, Merle."

"Your life ain't over, my friend. We're gonna work this thing out. What does your lawyer say?"

"Nothing. Hardly seen her but twice—maybe for five minutes each time. Says the sheriff's drawing up a bunch of charges." His eyes fixated on the floor. "My life's over."

Merle peered at Seth with narrowed eyes. "Good buddy, I'm

gonna ask you questions. Hard questions. And I want you to answer me with god's-honest truth. You hear?"

Seth turned his head to look at Merle. "What could you ask that's gonna make any of this right, Merle?"

"I dunno, Seth-er, but I gotta understand what was goin' on in your mind that morning we found the dead woman. And most important, how do you explain your size tens all over the woman's rug and porch, and how do you explain the fact that the neighbor 'cross the street says she saw you there?"

Head down, Seth returned his gaze to the floor.

Merle slapped the table hard with his big hand. "Seth! Earth to Seth Wilkins! Wake up! Soon Ha's gone! She's left you holdin' the bag for something you did not do!"

Slowly, Seth turned and faced Merle. Tears rolled from his eyes. "I give up. I'll tell you exactly what happened."

"From the beginning," Merle said, leaning his broad shoulders back in the chair, opening himself for the worst.

Seth wiped the back of his hand across his face and swallowed hard. "I was getting ready for work. My cell phone rang. It was Soon Ha. She was crying and just wild, talking so fast I couldn't hardly understand her. She said, 'Come and help me, Seth. My lady is dead. I come to work, and I find her dead on the floor. If I call the police, they'll send me away because my visa expired. I'm not here legal. I'll be deported. If they come here, they will think I killed her. Come help me, Seth!'"

Anguish radiated from Seth's sad eyes. "Does it say "stupid" when I say I went there because I love Soon Ha?"

"You *went* there *to the woman's house?*" Merle pushed his chair back from the table. "Listen up, man, I want all the facts. Start from square one an' don't leave nothin' out. I'm serious here, Seth. Start talking!"

"I drove there fast as I could. I didn't know what I was doing.

I guess I thought I was going to get Soon Ha and drive her somewhere safe. I don't know, I don't know…"

"So, what then?"

"I got there. Soon Ha was gone. I don't know why she wasn't there or where she went. I found the woman in the front room there. I was like walking in a dream or somethin'… decided to pick her up and put the body somewhere else. Dunno… maybe I thought it would look like someone other than Soon Ha was guilty because she couldn't lift someone as big as the woman, she had no car, no way to move her."

"How'd you move her?

"You know how. Like we learned in the army. Over the shoulder, like you're carrying a wounded buddy. I put her in my truck and put her there in the woods where I knew we would be mowing. Then it would look like somebody else dumped it there."

"Seth-er, I never thought you were a stupid man, but this beats all. What, again I ask, in the sam hill were you thinking?"

"That I was saving Soon Ha from being deported… or charged with murdering the poor woman."

Merle stood. "So now you're charged with murder." He stood and began pacing the small space; his big body filled the room. "If somebody could prove you didn't murder the woman, you'd still be charged with a bunch of other things." He threw his long arms up in the air. "I dunno what all—messin' with evidence, moving a dead body, not calling the authorities, 'aiding and abetting' something—I dunno what all." He paced back and forth. Neither man spoke for several minutes.

At last, Merle sat, leaned forward, and eyed Seth. "What time—*exact* time—did you get to the house? And what was the exact time you drove away? Think hard, this is important, might be part of your defense—when they get the time the woman died and all. Exact times, now."

In a subdued voice, Seth began. "Soon Ha called me a few minutes before six. She always went to work at the woman's house right around 6 a.m. I'd just gotten out of bed. So, I dressed real quick. Drove there—took maybe twenty minutes. Musta been at the house by 6:30. Took me less the ten minutes to lift the woman and get into the pickup."

"So, you drove away about 6:40?"

"At the latest."

"And you headed to our mowing route off Highway 36?"

"You know the rest. I raced home, cleaned up, met you to go to work."

"Seth-er, I see some good news here and some bad news. The good news is that maybe someone'll believe you when you say you didn't kill her. Bad news is you messed up big time by movin' her body and all. There's gonna be some hell-to-pay for that, for sure." Merle shook his head. "Gonna be some consequence."

Seth seemed relieved. "I know; I get that. I'll just confess everything, that I messed up." He took some deep breaths. "I know I'll go to jail for movin' the body… and for being stupid." He looked up at Merle. "What'd you say about the 'time of death?'"

"When they find out the time of death, they'll know you were there *after* she was killed, that she was dead already when you got there, so it's impossible for you to do the crime." Merle replied. "Lemme ask you one more question: We both saw how the woman's head was… you know. Did you see something heavy she mighta been hit with? Was there a weapon of some sort?"

"No… don't think so. There was lotsa blood where she was laying. A chair, dining room kind of chair, was laying on its side. A couple of wine glasses on the floor maybe." Seth wiped his sleeve across his face. "I wasn't looking around much. Just wanted to get the hell outta there."

Once again, Merle asked himself what to do next. *Gotta get this information to the DA. Somebody needs to interview Seth and get this on record. He did not kill Maybelle Jordan!*

Tanequa Milwood stood from her cluttered desk, tugged at her hip-length jacket, and extended her hand. "Good morning, Mr. Hucken, I believe you said you had some information for us."

"Ma'am, I sure appreciate you meetin' with me," Merle said as he leaned forward to shake the district attorney's hand. "I know it's kinda unusual for somebody like me to get himself involved here, but Seth Wilkins is my friend, he did not kill Ms. Jordan, and I can't sit by and let things just stand like they are."

"I understand, sir. You're the one who found Ms. Jordan's body."

"Yes, ma'am. Now, wanna mention that I tried talkin' to Seth's lawyer, but she doesn't return my calls. I've tried talkin' with the sheriff, but his deputy says he's too busy, so I sure hope I'm not stepping out of line here."

"Not at all, Mr. Hucken. If you have some information for us, I'm willing to listen." Tanequa Milwood dropped to her chair, folded her hands on the desk. She tipped her head as if assessing Merle. "Finding the body out there must have been terrible for you."

"Sure was. Followed by having my best friend jailed for something he did not do."

She gestured to an armchair. "How do you know that?"

Merle wedged into the small office chair and took a deep breath. "It's like this, ma'am… and what I'm thinking is nobody has questioned Seth thorough enough to get all the facts. I'm recommending—respectful like, 'cuz I'm not a detective, I'm just a guy who mows for a livin'—that one of your people talk with him again, because there's lots he didn't tell anybody."

"Sheriff Judd and his team questioned Mr. Wilkins. I have the report here. It says Mr. Wilkins pleads not guilty, but there's an eyewitness who saw him at Ms. Jordan's home, and furthermore, there are footprints matching his own footwear. His truck was gone over—there was Ms. Jordan's blood in the bed of the truck and on the tarp he used to cover her. Hard to explain away these facts."

"But ma'am, there's more to the story. Somebody needs to question Seth more, 'cuz he did not kill her, and he didn't give the real reason he was there—at the woman's house."

Tanequa Milwood shoved aside a tall stack of documents, pulled forward a legal pad, and uncapped a pen. "You say there's lots he did not say. What would that be?" She held up her hand as if to caution. "Before you tell me anything, Mr. Hucken, I advise you that anything you reveal regarding the homicide and the investigation can go on record, and it's very likely you'll be called to make a statement, then will be called to testify when a trial commences." She smiled wanly. In spite of being tired and her large brown eyes reflecting weariness, her face registered great interest.

"Okay, here's what I know, what Seth told me—he's crazy-nuts over the little Korean gal worked for Ms. Jordan. That morning Soon Ha called Seth right before six a.m., said she was at Ms. Jordan's, and she'd found the poor woman dead on the floor. She panicked because if she called police they'd find out she was here without papers—illegal like—and she was afraid they'd arrest her, she'd be deported. Now, I remind you, in all of this, Seth is head over heels with this girl, wants to marry her. His first thought is she's gonna be sent back to Korea, and he'll lose her. Now what he did next is really, really stupid, and he'll tell you what he did was stupid." Merle took a deep breath.

Tanequa Milwood was taking furious notes. "What happened next?"

"Seth got in his pickup, raced there like Dale Earnhardt. The back door to Ms. Jordan's was unlocked, he goes in, finds the poor dead woman."

"Where was—what's her name—Soon Ha?"

"Soon Ha Kim. Gone. Not there. Musta took off right after she called Seth."

The district attorney interrupted. "And at what time was this?"

"Near as he can figure, Seth says he got there at 6:30."

"At 6:30?" She pulled a document from a folder in front of her, lifted a page, and regarded it with a furled brow. "He's sure he arrived there at 6:30?"

"Yes, ma'am."

"So, what next? Soon Ha Kim was not there?"

"No, she took off—as a matter of fact, before Seth was arrested, we went to her family's restaurant looking for her, an' she was gone."

"Sorry to keep interrupting. Sheriff Judd took a statement from someone at the Korean woman's home; I have it somewhere… I believe they stated she'd returned to Korea, was no longer here." The district attorney wrote rapidly, then looked up at Merle with a puzzled expression. "What happened after he arrived there, and the Korean woman was gone?"

"Ma'am, this is the really stupid part, an' Seth knows this and will confess all this… he was so worried Soon Ha would be deported, he decides to move the body so's Soon Ha would not be questioned by police—who would find out she was not here legal-like and would deport her." Merle leaned forward and put his hands on the desk. "Ma'am, it all boils down to a poor guy who was so in love and so afraid he'd lose someone, that he made a really dumb mistake."

"Seth Wilkins told you this? That he was called by the Korean woman, he went to her aid, found her gone, but found the body of Ms. Jordan. He then moved the body." She scribbled on a legal pad. "Tell me at what time he left the scene."

"Yes, ma'am, like I said, he got there at about 6:30. He figures it took him ten, maybe fifteen minutes to sling the body over his shoulder, army-wounded-buddy-like, get it into his truck and drive off."

"So, he left the house at 6:45?"

"Yes, ma'am, he drove away at about 6:45. Drove to where we'd be mowin' later that day, knew we'd find the body, an' it'd make him look like he didn't know anything about the murder." Merle shook his head as if in disbelief. "I've known Seth all my life, and this is one for the books. The stupidest thing anybody coulda done." He looked up. "And he knows that, knows there's gonna be a consequence to movin' the body and all. He'll make a statement with all I just laid out here."

"Well, I must say, some of this does not fit with other parts of the investigation." She looked even more puzzled. "I'm thinking something's really irregular here." She again lifted the first page of a document and scrutinized the second page. "This doesn't make sense."

"What doesn't make sense, ma'am?"

The district attorney sat back in her chair and stared ahead. "There's just something I need to look into, to confirm." She stood. "Tell you what, Mr. Hucken, I'll do some due diligence, verify some information. Let me get back to you. You've been most helpful, and I truly thank you for coming in today. I'll give you a call when I've nailed down some details."

"Thank you, ma'am, for your time today. And please call me Merle."

Tanequa Milwood flashed a sincere and lovely smile. Merle couldn't help think she was a lot prettier when she smiled, but had the kind of job that keeps you studying and checking and working hard to make sure justice is done. The kind of job that doesn't give you lots of time to smile.

She extended her hand. "Thanks again, Merle. Seth Wilkins is lucky to have a friend like you."

CHAPTER 14

Merle drove home slowly and thought about his conversation with Tanequa Milwood. He reviewed over and over the D.A.'s reaction to the exact times Seth was at the house. What was wrong that made her keep looking at the second page of a document? What was the due diligence she needed to do?

He arrived home. Candy, dressed in exercise pants and an over-sized T-shirt, was diapering the baby. "Hi, sweetie, how'd your meeting go?"

"I feel sorta better 'bout things."

"How so?"

"Well, the D.A. strikes me as a real capable person, an' what strikes me best is she seems to care about the facts of the case, was real interested in what I told 'bout Seth being at the woman's house that morning. She asked when he arrived, when he left, took a bunch of notes. With her checking on things, I'm feeling more hopeful about Seth getting treated more fair."

"Oh, that's good to know," Candy said. She picked up the baby. "Say hi to Daddy. He's a real good friend to his Seth-er."

Merle chuckled, "Ms. Milwood said the same thing." He grabbed the phone. "Need to ask my boss something."

Merle dialed the office and asked to speak to his boss. "Jorge, this is Merle. Sorry to bother you, but what's the policy for a leave of absence?… Yeah, you're right, that finding a body has been hard… uh, huh… I think just a couple of days off, until we see what's what with Seth's charges, then I'll be back good as new… um, huh… Now you're sure, this is no trouble to anybody else, nobody's gonna hafta to work double time 'cuz me not bein' there?… Okay, well, I sure appreciate it. Talk to you first of next week. Thanks, Jorge."

Candy handed the baby to Merle. "I think that's a good idea, honey, to take off a few days."

Merle cradled Baby Maddy. "I hate missing work, sweetie. But, you know, something tells me I need to be available to help Seth and get this situation sorted out. Boss was real good about it, said not to worry."

"Oh look, Maddy," Candy said, looking out the window. "Granny Viv just drove up."

Holding the baby up, Merle stood at the window, took the baby's small hand in his, and waved to Viv who blew kisses back to the baby. She opened the door gently and smiled at the baby. "Hi all, and how's my girl?"

Viv dropped her purse and tote bag to a chair. "Merle, I just read in the funeral notices that Maybelle's memorial service is tomorrow. I think we should go and see who's there. Is that being too nosy?" Viv didn't wait for an answer. "Must say I'm kinda curious. I'll tag along with you. After all, I knew Maybelle in school, oh, so many years ago. Won't look funny for me to be there." She laughed out loud. "Tho' I haven't spoken to her for more than forty years!" She reached out for the baby. "An' 'sides, Merle, you went to school with Alvin Clegg. Would be nice for you to be there for him." She smiled a conspiratorial grin at Baby Maddy. "You think Granny Viv and your daddy oughta go see who's at that funny lady's funeral?" The baby babbled and giggled.

Merle thought hard. A mischievous look came across his wide, ruddy face. "You know, Viv, that's not a bad idea. Let's do it."

Merle tied his tie and donned his "wedding and funeral" jacket. The tan coat with its fine blue stripes pulled at the shoulders. The wide lapels were out of style. He could not button it.

"Honey, we need to get you a new jacket," Candy said. Today, she looked fresh and lovely, with a touch of lip gloss, her long shiny hair tied back with a gold ribbon. "This old one doesn't look comfortable."

"Sweetie, I go to something like today once in a blue moon. I'd rather save the money for Maddy's college fund. 'Sides, gonna lose some weight before I buy new clothes."

"Merle Hucken, I know better than to argue with you. One o' these fine days, I'm goin' out and buying you a new jacket. Savin' from the grocery money for that."

Merle said nothing, sucked in his stomach, and tried again to button the jacket.

Viv arrived, attired in her Sunday best—a blue-gray summer dress with a short jacket. Her silver-streaked hair was done nicely, and she wore her favorite pearl earrings—a gift from Candy's dad on their twenty-fifth wedding anniversary. "I'm ready when you are, Merle," she said.

Merle wedged into the driver's side of Viv's small car which, for the occasion, was a better choice than his rattling, groaning pickup.

Viv fastened her seat belt and said, "Guess there's no church service, 'cuz doubtful any self-respectin' preacher would show up to do a funeral for Maybelle." She laughed out loud. "Sorry, that wasn't nice, was it? Anyway, the service's at the mausoleum where they're putting her ashes."

"Who you think'll turn up for her sendoff?" Merle asked, laughing.

"Personally, I can't wait," Viv said, "to find out!"

They drove slowly through the cemetery and parked in front of a pink sandstone building. "I called this a mausoleum, but somebody said it's really s'posed to be called a columbarium—place where they put people's ashes," Viv said.

"Learn something every day," Merle said. "Hey, there's Alvin Clegg's BMW." He looked around. "Not many other cars here."

Viv counted five in all. "Remember, some people don't want to be known as May's friends. Understandable, they'd skip this event." She could not help giggling.

"Now, Viv," Merle said teasingly, "you're gonna keep a straight face through this. Don't embarrass us now."

Viv laughed her infectious laugh. "Yes, sirrrrrrr."

Tall rattan flower baskets filled with white roses, pink geraniums, and blue lobelia banked the location of Maybelle's niche. Alvin Clegg stood at the niche, and the small group of mourners formed a half circle. "You know any of these people?" Merle asked quietly.

Viv whispered, "A couple of guys from school days; don't know the women." She glanced around, "Some look familiar, but you know people change over the years—older, fatter, grayer."

"'Cept you, Granny Viv," Merle whispered back. "You're stayin' young as ever."

Gently, Viv shoved her shoulder into Merle's and smiled. "You are too kind, Mr. Hucken, but I'll accept that."

And then there was Sheriff Delbert Judd. His face ruddier than usual, he appeared to have been crying. He wore his own "wedding and funeral" suit, and it fit less well than Merle's. He'd easily gained 75 pounds—most of it around his midsection—since the last wearing, and he looked exceedingly uncomfortable. Viv moved to the sheriff's right and sensed the unmistakable scent of bourbon.

Alvin Clegg began the service. "I want to thank each and every one of you for coming today to honor my aunt, Maybelle Jordan. Aunt May was one of a kind. You could say she danced to the beat of a different drummer, but she was who she was. And she made no excuses. She was generous and caring; she helped me a lot during my early years, especially after my parents passed."

Alvin turned to four gentlemen to his right. "Now, I'd like to introduce the barbershop quartet from our local Stags lodge. These gentlemen requested that they sing a number in memory of Aunt May."

Alvin Clegg gestured to the men who crowded forward. A short, rail-thin man with very large ears spoke. "We were all friends to Maybelle, an' we'd like to sing a little hymn we know she liked." The speaker contrasted to others in that his coat was too large; his shirt collar gapped, exposing a huge Adam's apple. His extra-wide tie hung loosely, and the shoulders of his over-sized jacket stuck out. He removed a small round pitch pipe from his pocket and blew into it. The men leaned forward and hummed.

The hymn began with nice harmony, "Near thee, I'll always be…" As the song progressed, one gentleman's hangdog expression grew stressed and pale. He looked unkempt, his jacket needed cleaning, he hadn't shaved. His eyes teared up; soon his shoulders were shaking, and he was openly crying. Merle whispered to Viv, "Who's that guy who's lookin' like he's gonna pass out?"

Viv wanted to laugh out loud, but in a very controlled whisper, said, "That's Cal—we all went to school together."

"Cal who?" Merle whispered back.

"Calvin Medernicky."

"Medernicky?" Merle struggled to contain a giggle. "What kinda name…?"

As the hymn progressed, Calvin Medernicky became more and more bereft and ill-appearing, but the other singers carried on bravely. "All the storm of life pass me by…"

Suddenly he bolted away from the group and stumbled out the entrance. The unmistakable sound of someone retching fell on the ears of the mourners.

The hymn ended, each of the remaining men turned to Alvin and hugged him. One held on to him and muttered, "Not the same without Maybelle 'round here.'" The unmistakable sound of Calvin Medernicky vomiting continued; a bystander left to give him aid.

Embarrassed and mystified, Alvin took a few moments to recover. At last, he said, "I want to thank this fine group from the Stags Lodge. Yes, Aunt May was very fond of… that hymn." He cleared his throat and continued, "I'm sure most of you do not know that Aunt May's great-grandfather was a Civil War general. Aunt May collected and organized his letters and papers. She took loving care of his possessions knowing they had great historical significance. She asked me to help prepare the collection and often asked for my input and opinions. Now that the collection is intact and ready, I am donating it to the Southeastern Museum of Civil War History. It will be known as the Maybelle Elizabeth Jordan Memorial Collection. I'm sure it will be of great value to Civil War scholars and to historians who visit the museum. So, I'm pleased to honor Aunt May in this way. Now, I…"

Heads turned. A woman's loud voice, shouting from the parking area, yelled, "You go to hell, Maybelle Jordan, and take my goddam husband, Harold Cleland, with you!" A heavy woman, clearly inebriated, dressed in cut-offs and a hot pink T-shirt emblazoned with "What You Seez, Iz What's You Getz," staggered toward the stunned group. Her rounded layers of adipose tissue were molded into her all-too-tight and brief clothing.

Viv, turning to take in the sight, whispered to Merle, "Uh, oh, look who's payin' her respects." She held her hand to her mouth. "My lord, she's a ringer for the Michelin man—dressed southern."

Merle, struggling to keep a straight face, whispered, "Hush, Mama Viv, show some respect, please…" His belly—held tight in his jacket—betrayed him—rising and falling with stifled, hee-hee giggles.

Sheriff Judd turned, stumbled to his left, then—unsteadily— approached the shouting woman. "Now Charlene…" he began.

The woman tottered toward the bystanders, screaming, "Maybelle Jordan was a whore to end all whores! Burn in hell! Let 'er rot in hell! Good riddance!"

"Now Charlene," the sheriff slurred, "You go on home now…"

The woman careened to a halt in front of the wobbling sheriff. "Well, if it ain't the honorable Delbert Judd, comin' to pay his respects to his 'Wednesday-night gal.' You were there like regular, weren't you now, Delbert? Ever' Wednesday night with May." Her car keys laced in her fingers, she raised her hand and swung her arm in a circle. "We all know 'bout you, Delbert Judd." The keys flew from her hand striking the sheriff between his eyes. His hand flew up to his forehead; he staggered toward the woman, fell into her, and the two—belly-to-belly—crashed to the floor, knocking over one of the elaborate floral displays.

The handful of bystanders surged forward to assist and to assess the damage. One pulled away the rattan basket of flowers. The white roses and geraniums cascaded over and around the prostrate sheriff. Two men pulled the sheriff up and off the woman, brushed away the flowers and ferns from his clothing, and managed to get him standing again. His face bright red, he elbowed them away and staggered to his car. The men turned to the drunken woman and brought her to her feet. "Rot in hell, Maybelle Jordan," she slurred. "You just goddam rot in hell…"

Another man retrieved the woman's car keys. "I'll see Charlene gets home safe," he said. As the gentleman took her arm to lead her away, a shaky Calvin Medernicky—wiping his face with his jacket sleeve—could be seen walking unsteadily to his car. He was still weeping.

"Well," Alvin Clegg managed to say, "I don't know what else to say after that. But again, I thank you for coming; and if you could, please come back to my home for refreshments." He gestured to the parking area. "If you'd like to follow me to my home, my car is the BMW, dark blue, but please give me a moment to tidy up around Aunt May's resting place." Viv and another woman stepped forward to bring the flower basket to a standing position. They quickly snapped up the scattered flowers and tucked them in. "Thank you," Alvin Clegg said, steadying the basket. He dusted off his hands and said, "Okay, let's go have a glass of wine." Three cars, one carrying Merle and Viv, lined up behind the BMW and followed Alvin Clegg to his luxurious apartment.

As they drove, Viv asked, "You sure you wanna do this, Merle? We don't have to go, you know."

"I'm curious," Merle said, thoughtfully. "I kinda need to see what's what with Alvin."

"I do think Charlene Cleland and the boys from the Stags Lodge were the highlight of the day. Can't get much better than that."

Merle burst into his high-pitched, genial laugh. "That Medernicky fellow musta had a bad bellyache or something. I've seen him before, just can't remember where."

"Oh, he's around Fruitvale a lot. We all were in school same time. Always reminded me of the sheriff—same-type bald head, same pot belly, full of booze and bluster." She shook her head.

"Cal's a sad story. Never had many friends. Nowadays I think he spends his time at the Stag's Lodge. Inebriated, most all the time."

They arrived at their destination; Alvin waited out front for the group to gather. "Come on up," he said, holding the door open for the six people to enter. He escorted them to the elevator and into his apartment.

The group, subdued with very little conversation, gazed at the beautifully appointed space. Merle and Viv strolled to a floor-to-ceiling window. "Look Merle, you can see clear to the university over there." Viv pointed west.

"Yes," Alvin said, "I enjoy the view—when I saw this apartment, I knew this was the place for me."

Merle held a cup of coffee and ogled the display of small sandwiches and sweets on the oval dining table.

"Help yourself, Merle, you too Miss Vivian," Alvin said. The guests filled plates with elegant finger foods. There was more eating than talking.

"Alvin," Viv said, "I'm so impressed by you giving the Civil War things to the museum. So generous, and like you say, good for people to be able to see now and again."

"Yes, ma'am," Alvin said, sipping a glass of Chardonnay, "it's what Aunt May wanted."

"You told me a pistol was missing," Merle said through one gulp of a smoked salmon tea sandwich. "The thing ever turn up?"

"Not yet, but I haven't been able to get back into Aunt May's house to look—with all the investigation, crime-scene mess. Sheriff said I could get in there in a week or so. I'm sure it's there, just in a place I haven't thought to look… I think it's there."

CHAPTER 15

*W*HY AM I DOIN' THIS? Merle was lost in thought as his pickup chugged along. *I shouldn't even get involved here, I'm just a guy who mows, I don't have no business investigating anything... but I just gotta make sense of all this mess Seth's got himself in.*

He pulled the truck up to a stoplight and asked himself a slew of questions. *What did that drunk lady at the memorial service mean about the sheriff bein' at Maybelle's house? Was he seeing her like so many other men? One of her "gentlemen?"*

The car behind honked; the light had changed. Merle pressed the accelerator and pulled ahead. *Viv said to mention she and Edna Edgebert share cousins on her mama's side or some-such. Maybe then she won't throw me out for bothering her.*

He drew the pickup in front of Edna Edgebert's house, pulled keys from the ignition, and glanced across the street at Maybelle Jordan's house. *She does have a direct bead on ol' Maybelle's place. Easy to see she could tell who comes and goes and who can pull up the driveway and park 'round back...*

Merle headed to Edna's front door. He pulled in his belly the best he could, took some deep breaths, and rang the bell.

Edna Edgebert, her hair wound in 1970s-style rollers, opened the door immediately.

"Morning, ma'am," Merle said, taking off his cap, and

smoothing his spiky hair. "Sorry to bother you an' all, but I'm the friend of Seth Wilkins. My name is…"

"Merle Hucken. I know who you are. Was all in the paper, how you found that witch Maybelle's body out there off'n Highway 36."

"Yes, ma'am, an' my mother-in-law Vivian Smith says you'll are kinda related on her mama's side—cousins and all."

Edna Edgebert's pinched mouth softened for a moment. "Yes, I do believe we are related. Vivian Smith's your mother-in-law?"

"Yes, ma'am, I married her daughter, Candy."

"Candy Smith, real nice girl, friends with my niece Julie Beeth."

"Yes, ma'am. Reason I wanna talk to you is my friend Seth Wilkins is charged with murdering Ms. Jordan, and ma'am, I know it looks bad him bein' here and all the day she died, but he did not kill her, and I gotta just somehow convince Sheriff Judd of that fact. Would you mind if I just ask you a question or two?"

"Well, I dunno what I can tell you… Seth Wilkins was *here* that morning."

"Yes, ma'am, he was here, but Ms. Jordan was already dead when he got here."

"You don't say." Edna Edgebert's cross face took on a distinct look of interest. Her left eyebrow rose as if she wanted to know more. "Tell you what. Come on in here an' sit down some." She held the door open for Merle. He entered the dark and cluttered living room. Mildewed cartons lined one wall, and a stack of ancient vinyl records leaned at a crazy angle against the side of a sofa. A lamp with no shade rested on a pile of old newspapers.

Edna drew open heavy drapes. Dust motes fluttered in the morning sun. She pulled a short stack of magazines off a small armchair, then reconsidered. She turned to the sofa, shoved away a sleeping cat, and tossed aside a lumpy pillow. "You'd fit better here," she said. "Now how is it that Seth Wilkins came here that morning? If he didn't kill her?" She dropped heavily into the armchair. She grasped the chair arms, raised both eyebrows, and gave a smug, know-it-all look. "You know—his mama, Pearl, and Maybelle had a rowdy fight a night or so before. It sure as hell looked like he come there to finish the argument."

"Yes, ma'am." Merle sat carefully forward on the sofa, his long legs cramped behind a coffee table piled with dusty odds and ends including a bowl encrusted with old cereal and dried banana. "Looks bad that way, but the fact is he was called there by the young Korean lady who worked for Ms. Jordan, she'd found her dead, panicked, and asked for Seth to come help her. When he got there, Soon Ha was gone, then he did a stupid thing—he moved the body out there to the side of Highway 36. He admits he did that—moved the body—stupid thing to do, but he did not kill her."

Edna listened carefully to all Merle had to say. "Who killed her then?"

"I don't know. Did you see anyone else there—during the night?"

"Well, Alvin Clegg was there the night before—evening, it was. He carried out some boxes. He was parked right out front." She fiddled with a hair roller and added, "He and May were getting along better those last days."

"What, ma'am, do you mean by them getting along better?"

Edna Edgebert folded her arms. "Well, you know Maybelle was very hard on Alvin. I can't tell you how many times I heard her yelling awful things at him."

"Like what, ma'am?"

"Oh, she had all kinda names for him. She'd yell, 'you're nothin' but a sissy-boy, a fancy boy, a girly boy.' I mean Alvin was kinda different, you know, but he was never a bad kid."

Edna Edgebert looked thoughtful. "I heard her yell at him,

'You're so light in your loafers, you're just gonna float away!'"
Edna shook her head. "Maybelle was right mean to Alvin, now
that I think about it." She removed a loose roller from her dyed
brown hair. "But he was never rude back to her, that I recall."

"So he was at the house in the evening—say what time, you
think?"

"About eight, before eight-thirty. Still evening light out. I
was outside watering my hostas."

"Now, after that visit from Alvin, was there anyone else at
the house later? Like one of her gentleman friends?"

Edna Edgebert took her time to think through Merle's question. She pulled rollers one-by-one from her hair and piled them
in her lap. Merle waited patiently.

"Well, it was a Wednesday night. And Delbert Judd comes
there ever' Wednesday night, 'round ten, ten-thirty and stays till
middle of the night. I know 'cuz some Wednesday nights I go to
the movies with Eloise Carteret, and we'd come home, and the
sheriff's car be there—right around midnight."

"So, he was there the night before Maybelle was found—at
about that time?"

"Well, now, I was not out to a movie that night, and so I can't
say I exactly saw him there that night. But, like I say, he was
there ever' Wednesday night, so he more-than-likely was."

"But you didn't actually *see* him or his car that night?"

"No, sir, can't say as I did. But I sure did see Alvin there in
the earlier evening, and I sure did see your buddy Seth Wilkins
there the next morning." She yanked the last roller from her hair.
"An' I sure did see Seth's mama yelling at Maybelle Jordan!"

Merle drove away from Edna Edgebert's with more questions
than ever. He needed to clear his mind, let things settle, review
the facts.

He glanced at the dashboard of his pickup and grabbed the dry-cleaning ticket for his black jeans. "I'll get the jeans then head home. Maybe everything Ms. Edgebert told me, what Seth told me, what the district attorney sort of told me… will make sense later."

He pulled up to Jimmy Chung's establishment and parked. As he pulled the key from the ignition, he noticed the "Closed" sign hanging in the entrance window. "Not Sunday; why's he closed?" Merle approached the door and turned the handle. It was open. "Maybe Jimmy forgot to turn over the sign…"

Expecting Jimmy to greet him in his usual jovial manner, Merle waited. At last, he called out, "Hey, Jimmy, need those jeans for the big doin's at the White House!"

No answer for several minutes. Merle glanced around the usually immaculate shop. Cardboard boxes were randomly stacked in front of the counter, the floor was gritty and needed sweeping, the counter was cluttered with tags and receipts. Merle couldn't help notice things looked disorganized and out of place.

He called out again, "Hey Jimmy, you closed today?"

Jimmy Chung, his usual pleasant expression replaced with a worried look of consternation, erupted from behind a carousel of film-wrapped clothing. He snatched the ticket from Merle's hand. "Hey Merle, got your jeans. Just a sec. . ."

He disappeared momentarily to the rear of the shop, and once again burst through hanging garments with dry-cleaned jeans in hand. He pushed the garment at Merle. "No charge, Merle. On the house," he said breathlessly. "Real busy. Can't chat much. I… I… gotta big order to do." He retreated as rapidly as he had appeared.

Merle was speechless. He turned slowly and walked to his pickup. *What's goin' on here? Never saw Jimmy like this. He's always had time to talk. Never wasn't friendly and full of fun.*

Merle slid into his pickup. *Something's just crazy here. What's going on?*

CHAPTER 16

MERLE ENTERED THE DOUBLEWIDE AND placed his newly cleaned jeans over a chair. Candy—dressed in jeans, her hair done nicely, a touch of lipstick—came from the baby's room with Maddy in her arms. She looked fresh—happier, more interested in life. "Hey, honey, got your jeans, did you? How's Jimmy Chung?"

Merle took a minute to answer. "Jimmy was nervous-like. Rattled. Never seen 'im like he was today. Worries me. I'd almost think I'd done somethin' to offend him, but I know I didn't." Merle opened the fridge and peered in. He looked up at Candy. "Think I'll go back tomorrow, and just check in to see what's what with Jimmy." His gaze returned to the contents of the refrigerator. "Can I have one of these yogurt cups?"

"'Course, honey, a healthy choice—low fat, low sugar," Candy replied, gently rocking Maddy. "You don't think he maybe didn't want to talk about the tattooed Koreans at the barbecue place again? He said those guys scare him."

"Dunno. Just dunno," Merle pulled open the top of the container and plunged a spoon inside. "Heard some interesting stuff from Edna Edgebert…" He directed the spoon into his mouth. He mumbled through a mouthful of strawberry yogurt, "Stuff about the sheriff and Alvin Clegg."

"What stuff?"

"They both were at Maybelle Jordan's the night before she

died. At least Alvin was there for sure, early evening of the night before. The sheriff is always there every Wednesday night, till way late, 'tho Ms. Edgebert didn't actually see him that night. But she seemed to be real sure he was Maybelle's 'Wednesday-night guy.'"

"Would that make them suspects of murdering poor Maybelle?"

"Dunno. I'll have me another talk with Ms. Milwood. Wanna ask her what she thinks."

For the rest of the afternoon and early evening, Merle—his mind spinning myriad directions—worked around the house, trimmed the bushes outside, swept the porch and front walk, organized recycling, took some trash to the dump. All the while, he mulled over Edna's news: *Maybelle treated Alvin badly—but they were getting along better just before she died. What did that mean? And most confusing, Sheriff Judd was—possibly, likely— at Maybelle Jordan's late the night before she was found dead.*

And he had an important question: *Isn't that something the sheriff should have divulged as part of the investigation? Too bad Edna, in all her nosiness, wasn't eyewitness to his visit.*

Later, Merle brought home take-out dinner: Mr. Smutt's-style barbecue pork, cole slaw, hush puppies. Candy set the table and poured sweet tea over ice cubes in big glasses. "Enjoy this, honey, 'cuz we're eating healthier foods from now on."

Merle looked up from his plate with a dark look. "No more 'cue?"

"Doesn't mean we won't eat foods we love, Merle. Just won't eat it as often. It'll be a real treat when we do. We're gonna have more fresh veggies, no fried stuff. We gotta slim you down, keep you healthy."

"Doesn't sound fun, sweetie." He gave his best sad look. "You tryin' to punish me?"

"No, I don't want you to get diabetic, get sick. I love you too much to let that happen."

Merle smiled at Candy. "You know best, sweetie."

After dinner, Candy sat at her computer and web surfed. She read on-line reports of the Maybelle Jordan homicide. "Doesn't say anything new about the murder investigation," she wondered out loud. "Is the investigation complete, you think, honey?"

Merle, stretched out in his recliner, looked up from a sports magazine. "Not sure. Not real confident with Sheriff Judd runnin' things. He thinks he's got a slam-dunk against my buddy Seth. And he won't listen. My only hope is Ms. Milwood, the D.A., can get the real facts."

Candy turned from the computer. "The big question is 'who killed Maybelle Jordan?' We know Seth is not guilty, that's for darn sure. Let's list the suspects." She pointed her thumb as number one. "Seth's Korean girlfriend—who nobody seems to be able to locate." She pointed her index finger. "Two, one of May's 'gentlemen.' Three, a disgruntled wife or girlfriend; four, Pearl Wilkins. Anybody else?"

Merle took a moment to answer. "I hate to even think this—Alvin Clegg? Ms. Edgebert said Maybelle was real mean to Alvin, called him names—if she'd treated Alvin bad, maybe he'd a reason to do her in, maybe just couldn't take the abuse anymore. But, on the other hand, Ms. Edgebert said they were getting along better lately." He pulled himself from the recliner, stretched, and yawned. "I dunno—I'm just a guy who mows for a livin.' What do I know about investigatin' a murder?" He bent over to kiss Candy. "I don't know why, but I'm still thinking about Jimmy Chung. He was not himself today."

They went to bed about 10:30; Merle could not sleep. He rolled over to look at Candy who slept soundly. Moonlight filtered through a slatted shade and gleamed on her shiny auburn hair spread out over her pillow. *I'm the luckiest man in the world.*

Viv says Candy's 'baby blues' are going away. I'm getting my pretty lady back. I so want her to be a happy lady. He wanted to put his arms around her and to hug her, but she needed sleep; Maddy was an early riser—often at 5:30 a.m. He rolled over, still thinking. He glanced at the clock: 12:15.

He mulled over his visit with Edna Edgebert, his talk with the DA, the curt and rigid mindset of Sheriff Judd. *An' what the heck's goin' on with the Korean barbecue guys? What happened to Soon Ha?* The questions multiplied, magnified. Restless, he rotated his big body, disturbing Candy. She snorted and mumbled.

This is no good. Can't sleep. I'll keep Candy up... Moving as slowly and quietly as he could, he got up, pulled jeans off a chair and grabbed a T-shirt. He dressed in the living room and tiptoed out. His shoes were on the porch; he pulled them on and headed to the pickup. *What the sam hill am I doin'?*

The pickup seemed to start and drive itself. With few cars out at that time of night, Merle—hardly realizing—quickly found himself in the parking lot behind the Joh Eun barbecue restaurant. As he drove around the side of the building—which was dark now, closed—he hadn't the presence of mind to cut the lights. He pulled up near the restaurant's back door. The door flew open, and light fell on three figures in the doorway—two slim, fit men and one portly figure with short arms and a wide belly. Merle suppressed a moment of panic but drove slowly around the building and down the street. He stopped at a stop-light a few blocks away when a car raced up behind. The light changed. Merle pulled ahead, and the car behind tailgated, rode the bumper of Merle's old pickup. *Who is that guy?* He snapped shut the locks on the doors and tried to be calm. *They gonna follow me all the way home? Can't go home. Can't have them near my home, my Candy, my baby.*

He calmly drove the speed limit; all the while the mystery

car dogged him from behind. He knew he'd be passing the neighborhood fire station. He pulled a quick right turn, drove up to the station, and hesitated under the floodlights surrounding the building. The car behind him burned a U-turn and stopped across the street away from a street lamp.

Hope they know better than to cause trouble here at the fire station. Soon, a firefighter—as tall as Merle—exited a side door and strode to the driver side of Merle's pickup. "Help you, sir?" he began, but suddenly realized he knew Merle. "Hey, Merle Hucken, how ya doin'? We've missed you 'round here. How's Seth? And by the way, why you out this time of night?"

The engine of the car across the street suddenly revved up and sped away, screeching tires.

The firefighter looked confused. "What's with those guys?" he asked.

Merle took a couple of deep breaths and greeted Jeremy Higgins, firefighter and acting chief of the Fruitvale Fire Department.

"Hey, Jeremy, just some kids out joyriding, thought it'd be fun to tailgate and bug me. Now they're speeding, so maybe a trooper'll catch 'em somewhere on down the road." Merle extended his hand. "What's up, Jeremy. I've missed helpin' out you guys."

"You doin' okay, Merle, since finding that woman out there? An' we can't believe they locked up Seth for her murder. They for sure got the wrong guy."

"That's for sure. I told Sheriff Judd a bunch of times they got the wrong guy. Kills me Seth's sittin' in jail for something he did not do."

"Askin' again, Merle, what the heck you doin' out here this time of night?"

"Remembered our baby girl was outta diapers. Headed up to the convenience store—open all night, you know." Merle's heart was beating out of his chest, questioning himself as to why he was actually out this late at night, and now lying to a friend.

"So, hey, Merle," Jeremy asked, "you gonna get back doing volunteer firefighting? Like I said, we've missed you—and Seth, too."

"As soon as we can get Seth cleared of these charges. The district attorney's looking into things so I'm tryin' to keep hopeful—that they'll find Seth innocent. Yep, I've missed the firefighting scene—yearly training is comin' up soon, isn't it?"

"Sure is. I'll call you with the exact dates. And we learned that they're makin' us all weigh in now, checkin' to see if we're carrying too many pounds for our height." Jeremy glanced down at Merle's belly.

"Uh, oh. I'm in trouble…"

"Lots of us guys have gotten out of shape. We're putting in a treadmill and cooking healthier stuff. Sure do miss the fried catfish ol' Norm Walker cooked for us when he's on duty. Now he's doing kale and weird stuff like that."

"Candy's after me to lose weight. Know I gotta do this. Be sure to let me know when the training's happening, and just as soon as this thing with Seth is resolved, I'll be back on volunteer duty."

Jeremy chuckled. "You remember that nice old lady we saved last year. She forgot to turn off the stove, and the kitchen caught fire?"

"Sure do. She doin' okay?"

"Ran into her at the Piggly Wiggly the other day, she recognized me, and asked about you." Jeremy gently poked Merle and laughed. "Know what she said? 'Where's that gentle giant, Merle? The big man who found my little Chester out in woods—so frightened and cold—the night my house caught fire?'"

Merle laughed his squeaky laugh. "Oh, yeah—Chester was her little terrier took off while we were hosing down the house.

She was real worried about that little dog. When we caught a break, I headed out behind the house and found the poor little guy under some bushes."

"Yeah, anyway, the lady wanted me to remember her to the 'gentle giant.'"

Both men chuckled. "Be sure to let me know about that training, Jeremy."

"I'll do that," Jeremy answered. "Stay safe, Merle. Let me know what happens with Seth."

Merle drove home—all the while glancing back to see if the mystery tailgater was near. He pulled in behind the doublewide and waited. The neighbor's porch light still burned and helped to illuminate the back and side yards. He turned his wide shoulders to look around before getting out of the pickup. *All clear.* He hurried around, removed his shoes, and unlocked the front door.

Questions raced through his head: *Was that Sheriff Judd with the Korean guys? Why at this time of night? And who in heaven's name was following me?*

CHAPTER 17

T HE NEXT MORNING, SUNDAY, MERLE awakened to bright sun slanting through the shades of their small bedroom. Candy stood at the doorway. She smiled. "Hey, sleepy-head, you slept in this morning. You want some breakfast? All-white egg omelet, whole wheat toast, fresh fruit?"

Merle sat up in bed. His heart fluttered as he thought of his visit to the restaurant, the fact he'd been seen there—in the middle of the night with no earthly business or reason to be there. And who was driving the car that sped up and followed him? He set aside his worries and looked up, as always, transfixed by Candy's creamy skin, her rosy dimpled cheeks, her smiling green eyes. "Ah, sweetie," he pretended to moan, "I need me some Krispy Kremes. It's Sunday…" He gave Candy his best sad-sack look.

He could tell he was breaking down her resistance. "Well, it is Sunday," she said, "Just this once, okay? You enjoy those calorie-alleys because no more after this. Okay?"

"You got it, sweetie!" He jumped out of bed, shaved and dressed, grabbed the keys to the pickup. He hurried around to the pickup; a paper fluttered on the windshield. "What's this?" He lifted a windshield wiper, carefully pulling the paper away. He stared at Asian writing. *This in Korean?* Seemed so, from the few symbols he was acquainted with…

He pulled a business card from his wallet and dialed his

phone. He left a message: "Hey, Dave, this is Merle Hucken. We talked a while back at the Korean barbecue joint. You said to call if I needed to know anything Korean. Well, I got a message on my windshield this morning, and I think it's written in Korean. Could you translate it? Kinda worries me. Could you meet me at Hardee's in the next, say, 30 minutes or so? I'll grab us some coffee and wait there. Geez, I know this is real inconvenient, Sunday morning and all. If you can't meet me this morning, then please call me as soon as you can. Here's my number…"

About fifteen minutes later, Merle pulled into Hardee's parking lot to find—not David Evans, but Karina Evans waiting for him. "Hey, Merle, let me see it." Merle handed her the paper and waited. "This is bad, Merle. Short translation is: 'You ask too many questions. You and wife and baby are in danger.'"

Merle's clear blue eyes widened; his usually rosy face turned pale. "What should I do?"

"Get to the district attorney as quickly as you can. Tell her you've been threatened. They'll put an SBI agent on it. Right away, Merle. I'd help more, but that's all I can do—and I have to leave now." She turned and strode to her car. "Call the DA now!"

Merle stood silent, numb. His heart pounded; he was sweating. *Candy and Maddy are in danger. Ohmygosh, it's all my fault! First, it's my best friend Seth, now my family?* He walked zombie-like to his pickup and walked right into Sheriff Delbert Judd.

The sheriff's wide-frame blocked the driver-side door. He leaned against the pickup with one leg crossed over the other, his arms folded across his belly. "Morning, *Co-lum-bo.* I got some orders for you: Back off from whatever *am-a-teur* detective playin' you're playin' at. I told you once an' I'll tell you again: Let us professionals deal with this."

"Sir, I'm just lookin' out for my friend, Seth Wilkins, who's falsely accused…"

Angry, the sheriff screwed up his face and spat words through tight lips. "And listen up, fat boy, I'm tellin' you one more time… you back off, or I'll see you're charged with obstruction of justice!"

Merle drew up his full height and looked down at the blustering sheriff. "Sir, you don't worry me none. I've already been threatened this morning… and in Korean." He gently shoved the sheriff from the pickup door.

The sheriff turned bright red, said nothing, and stormed away.

Merle sat at the wheel and dialed Candy. "Sweetie, do something for me; I got side tracked and haven't been to Krispy Kreme yet. Do this for me: Lock all the doors and don't go out of the house, okay?… I know, I know… I don't mean to scare you; it's just that something weird's goin' on, and I'm just being careful. Probably isn't anything, but you stay inside, okay? Be home in a minute."

He rifled through his wallet for the DA's number. He left a message, mentioned Karina Evans's warning, asked to see her as soon as possible.

Merle raced across the street to the Krispy Kreme store, grabbed two boxes, and raced home. As he turned into the narrow drive alongside the doublewide, he noticed a tan car parked nearby. A single individual sat at the wheel, his elbow out the open window. *Must be someone visiting the Green's next door,* Merle thought as he unlocked the front door.

He found a worried Candy waiting for him. "What's happened?"

Merle opened a box of doughnuts, and through mouthfuls, mumbled, "I called and left a message for the DA. I'm sure she'll call. Let's stay cool. Everything's gonna be okay, sweetie. Don't worry. I'm here, and we'll just wait to hear from her."

Within minutes, Tanequa Milwood called. Before Merle could say anything, she said, "Merle, we're on it. An SBI agent is outside your house. Just be cautious now. Stay close to home; caution your family."

"Yes, ma'am, Karina Evans, a lady I met who knows Korean, translated the note."

"Yes, I know about the note. Who all have you talked to about Seth's case?"

Merle spoke rapidly telling the DA about his visit to Edna Edgebert, her comments about Alvin Clegg and the possibility of the sheriff being at Maybelle's. He gave details about his driving to the restaurant and seeing three men at the back door. He did not mention his concerns about Jimmy Chung.

The DA listened carefully. She reviewed and questioned each detail. Merle could tell she was taking notes.

Merle thanked the DA for her call. She once again assured Merle he and the family were being protected by the SBI, but to be very cautious.

When he ended the phone call, he said out loud, "Wonder how she knew about the note on the windshield. An' how'd they get the guy watchin' the house here so fast?"

"What, honey?" Candy asked. "What note are you talking about? When was it you saw some guys at the Korean restaurant?"

"Just runnin' by details for the DA, an' she said they have an SBI watching the house, just to keep us safe. Not to worry..." He grabbed another doughnut. "You mind if I finish this box of Krispy Kremes?"

CHAPTER 18

THE NEXT MORNING, CANDY AROSE early as usual to nurse Maddy. She lifted a living room shade to see a car parked at the front of the house. The SBI agent was on duty. Relieved, she settled on to the sofa and clicked on the television. She kept the volume low; Merle was still sleeping.

Maddy was fussy. "Shush, sweet baby girl, mama's movin' fast as can be," she cooed to the baby. The baby soon settled down, and Candy held her gently and smiled down at her. "Sweet baby, mommy's here…"

Candy glanced up at the television. "Breaking News" flashed across the screen. The morning anchor, her hair done in cascading ringlets, her make up perfect, her deep V-neck blouse showing the right amount of cleavage announced in a matter-of-fact voice, "Well-known business owner, Jimmy Chung, was found dead last evening in the workroom of his dry-cleaning establishment… Police suspect foul play, are treating Mr. Chung's death as a homicide…"

Candy leaped from the sofa, jolting the baby who began to cry. "Merle, Merle, come here! Wake up, Merle! Oh, this is awful! Merle! Merle!"

Merle bolted from the bed. "What? Are the Koreans outside? What?"

Candy, frantic, pointed to the television in the living room.

"Look! Look! Jimmy Chung is dead!" Maddy was red-faced and screaming.

Merle hiked up his pajama bottoms and stood barefoot in front of the TV. "Ohmygosh, Jimmy Chung. Good man, Jimmy Chung. Not Jimmy Chung," Merle moaned as he listened for more details. Merle was incredulous, heartbroken, at a loss for words. "What in the sam hill is goin' on here?" He paced back and forth. "Candy? Candy? Where'd you go?"

The baby was quiet now, still nursing, but Candy was back in bed, the baby at her breast. Merle waited until the baby seemed finished, then gently lifted the sleepy Maddy from Candy's arms. Candy rolled over and pulled the covers around her head.

"You okay, sweetie?"

Candy was weeping.

"Talk to me, sweetie," Merle said softly. "I'm sad too. We've lost a good friend."

Candy sobbed, "Poor Marie, losing her wonderful husband, such a terrible thing, to be murdered… to…" Candy screamed out, through choking sobs, "She's such a good person. She came to see me. She helped me so much. She doesn't deserve this!"

Merle looked down at the sleeping baby, his heart aching, "We don't know why bad things happen to good people," he said through tears of his own. He knew the best thing he could do was to let Candy be, to let all this bad news settle. "I'll let you rest, sweetie. We'll talk later."

Merle closed the bedroom door quietly and sank to the sofa in the living room. *Uh, oh. Just when Candy's coming out of the 'baby blues'—now this happens. This is all my fault. I shoulda never messed with any of this.*

Worried, his stomach turning, he cradled the sleeping Madison Hucken in his arms. *I've put my girls at great risk. Who's stupid now?*

Merle stayed close to home. Since the murder of Jimmy

Chung, he was frantic about the safety of his family. The un-marked vehicle parked outside his home gave some comfort, but his heart pounded, his mind raced. He worried.

CHAPTER 19

L ATE-MORNING OF THE NEXT DAY, Merle dialed Pearl. "Morning, Ms. Wilkins, wondered if you have any news 'bout Seth. His attorney have any news?"

Pearl exhaled cigarette smoke. "Well, Seth's still in the hoosegow. Yeah, I talked with that child-lawyer who's s'posed to defend Seth. She says Sheriff Judd's maybe gonna try me as an accessory to murder. That it might look like I was gettin' revenge against that witch Maybelle Jordan." She coughed. "Whadya think of them apples?" She coughed again.

"Not very much," Merle said. "Did Seth's lawyer say anything about the time they know Ms. Jordan died? The time of death? And have they questioned Seth again since the first time they put him in jail?"

"No and no."

Merle looked up to see Viv arrive, closing the door gently behind her.

"Ms. Wilkins, I'm gonna try to speak to the district attorney. I'll let you know if she says anything important. Talk to you later… you take care now."

Merle clicked off the phone. He stared at Viv who was tearful, had been crying. "I am so sad for the Chung family," she said.

"I'm just sick," Merle breathed out. "And… I dunno, Granny Viv, Candy's back in bed. She's all sad and depressed again. Not only because of Jimmy Chung, but this whole thing with the Koreans threatening me and the SBI guy sittin' out front. Has us all freaked out." Merle shook his head and tossed his phone on the sofa. He threw open his wide arms. "How'd I get involved in all this mess? All this is so hard on Candy."

Viv placed her handbag in a narrow closet and hung up her sweater. She took a tissue from her pocket and dabbed at her eyes. "You care about people, Merle. You're an honest, good man—and when you see something wrong, you help to fix it. There's a lot of wrong goin' on right now—especially with Jimmy Chung bein' murdered."

Merle held his hands to his head. "I'm just a guy who mows… shouldn't try to fix somethin' like Seth being charged wrong. This isn't something in my control."

Viv eased down in a chair across from Merle. Neither spoke for several minutes.

Viv cleared her throat. "But when there are things *in* your control, you always help, Merle… like after the hurricane hit, you were out there with the chainsaw and got the street cleared and people's walks cleared. You pulled that huge branch off Green's porch, sawed it up in no time, and hauled it away."

"That was easy, Viv, not something like this." Merle lay back on the sofa. "This is more than a guy coulda ever bargained for…"

"Merle, what I'm sayin' here is… you help people. And now, you won't stand aside and let Seth be convicted of murder when you know he did not do it. So that's why you've done what you've done. For all the right reasons." She blew her nose. "Tell you what, Merle, we're gonna just pull up our socks and move on. Gotta do some things for the Chung family now. I'm gonna do some cookin' to take to them."

Viv stood, bent over the playpen, and hoisted Baby Maddy. "Hey, pretty girl, Granny's here." The baby cooed and smiled.

"It all sounds right when you say that, Viv, but this isn't as easy as sawin' up branches and cleanin' up after a storm. This is real hard on Candy; I'm worried about what this is doin' to her…"

"Merle, I think Candy's stronger than we think. Some women go through a depression after childbirth. I talked to Candy's OB, and she suggested some counseling and treatment. Candy'll pull out of this; we just have to help and be patient." She shifted the baby to her hip. "Did you know Marie Chung came to see her last week? They had a long, long talk. I do think Candy has been much better since then."

"Candy has been better," Merle replied. "You know, Viv, I'd do anything to help Candy."

"Yes, that's for sure, Merle, but here's somethin' else I've been thinking… Candy's a real smart, smart lady. She's one of those women who maybe needs more than keeping house and tending babies. This doublewide is right nice, a nice home, you make a decent livin' for her and Maddy… but for someone like Candy, it's very confining. She needs a wider world, Merle. And it's nothing against you—she adores you. She just needs to be 'out in the world,' so to speak."

Merle listened, shook his head in agreement. "I know for darn sure I'm getting cabin fever being in this doublewide all the time…"

Viv shifted the baby to her other hip. "One of these days, I'm gonna offer to take care of Maddy full-time, so's Candy can go back to work. I really think that'll help some of this feeling so down and blue." Maddy giggled and blew bubbles. "Yes, sweet girl, Granny Viv's sayin' your mommy's a smart lady and needs to get outta this house!"

"When things calm down one of these days. Maybe we'll get back to normal, I'll get back to work, Seth'll be proved innocent…"

"We'll think positive," Viv responded.

Merle stood and wrapped his big arms around Viv and the baby. "I sure do appreciate you, Vivian Smith. Thank you for all you do for us."

"Helping you and Candy helps me, Merle." Viv patted his arm, pulled away, opened the fridge. Still holding Maddy, she peered in and shuffled things. "What we got to eat in here, sweet baby? Let's fix your mommy a nice lunch." She turned to Merle. "Go see if you can get Candy to come join us."

Merle tiptoed into the bedroom. "Sweetie, Granny Viv's fixin' lunch. Come be with us."

"Not hungry," Candy mumbled. "Tired, wanna sleep some more."

Merle parked his bulk on the edge of the bed. "But, sweetie, I need you to help me," he said in his best voice that always tugged at Candy. "Need you to Google me a bunch of things. To find out more about Alvin Clegg. I need your help to get Seth outta jail." He stroked her hair. "An' Granny Viv says we need to get some stuff ready to take to the Chung family." He bent down and kissed her on the cheek. "Please."

Candy flopped her arm over Merle's thigh. "I'll do a couple of things, then I'm going back to bed."

"You're my sweetheart, Candy Hucken."

Merle and Viv heard Candy showering. She came to the table dressed in clean pajamas but wearing her security blanket, the ratty old velour robe, the sleeve edges frayed with loose threads. The bronze-orange color of the ancient garment complemented her clear skin, auburn hair, and green eyes. She plopped down and pushed away a thick turkey sandwich. "Not hungry, Mama."

"S'okay, darlin,'" Viv said. She removed the sandwich and placed it in the fridge. She returned to the table and sat across from Candy. She took Candy's hands in hers. "Sweetheart, you know, you are my beautiful baby girl—just like sweet Madison is your beautiful baby girl. We want our baby girls to be happy, to have a happy and content life."

Candy burst into tears, pulled her hands from Viv's, and covered her eyes. Viv continued, "There is help out there for how you're feeling right now, and your good Dr. Fraser has the treatments and sources for help. You know that… and remember what Marie told you… about how she went through something like this…"

Candy wept. Merle, who had been sitting quietly on the sofa, wept as well. He held his broad hand to his forehead to hide the tears.

Viv, speaking calmly, quietly, continued. "Right now, someone else is worse off than us. We have to be strong for our dear friend, Marie Chung, and for her boys, and for Jimmy's dad 'cuz they're grieving; they've lost the light of their lives." Viv stood, grabbed tissues, and handed them to Candy and Merle. She dried her own tears.

"Jimmy's funeral will be sometime next week—when Marie's mother and other family arrive from Korea. Let's be strong for them. I need to fix up some food for all the family and visitors who'll pass through their house. Will you help me do that—for Marie?"

Candy stood from the table and retreated to the bedroom. Merle stood, and Viv hugged him. "Try not to worry so much, Merle. This too shall pass," Viv whispered.

Forty-five minutes later, Candy emerged from the bedroom. She was dressed in neat jeans and a fresh starched blouse. She wore a pair of new sandals, a change from the run-down felt slippers she'd worn for weeks. Her long hair was held back with brass-colored barrettes. She had put on makeup, emphasizing her long lashes and curvy lips.

She settled at the computer. "What you need me to Google, Merle?"

Merle and Viv exchanged glances. Each struggled to control another flood of tears.

Merle bent down and kissed Candy. "Thank you, sweetie." He took a moment to rein in a torrent of emotion. He swallowed hard, took a deep breath. "See if you can find more about that museum Alvin's donating the papers and all to—it's over at Atlanta—I wanna know if the stuff's on exhibit or when they'll put it up there. Can you do that?"

"Give me a few minutes." In short order, Candy found the museum and the name of the curator. "Here's the guy to call," she said. "Anything else right now?"

"This is great, sweetie, thank you."

Candy picked up the baby. "I'll bathe Maddy. When I'm done, I'll check other things you need." She cradled the baby and headed to the baby's room. "Hey, baby girl, let's get you all prettied-up."

Merle looked at Viv and managed a smile. Still emotional, his flushed face registered gratitude, relief, powerful love for the women in his life. He took a moment to recover, then dialed the number. He spoke in his best business-like manner: "Yes, ma'am, I'm interested in the Maybelle Jordan Civil War collection that's been donated there. Wondered when it's gonna be put on exhibit and all. Could I speak with your curator, Mr. Wilson, about that?"

Merle was put through. "Yes, sir, it's the Maybelle Jordan Civil War collection and all—that's brought there by her nephew Alvin Clegg." Merle sank to the sofa and took in the news that the curator had no knowledge of any such Maybelle Jordan Civil War memorabilia, that he knew no Alvin Clegg, that he was very sorry he could not be of help.

Merle ended the call with more questions than ever. "Why? Could it be that it just hadn't been brought there? But Al said it was all a done deal." He redialed the curator. He apologized for bothering him again, but said, "Lemme ask you this, if you had an important collection of Civil War stuff, and you wanted to sell it, where would you take it? Locally, I mean."

The curator's answer was "Luthely's in Greenville."

Rather than wait for Candy to finish bathing the baby, Merle tried his hand at Googling for info about Luthely's. It was easier to let Candy do this; she was so adept at the computer.

At last, after great trial and error and much frustration expressed as "dad-gum-mit," and "shoulda learned this stuff, shoulda took a computer course," Merle found a phone number for the auction house known at Luthely's.

Once again, he dialed up his business voice and said to the woman on the phone, "I'm interested if you have anything comin' up soon with Civil War memorabilia. Up for auction? Real au-then-tic kind of stuff?" He'd wished he'd used a better word than "stuff." He remembered the word "artifacts," too late.

The answer: "Yes, Mr. Alvin Clegg's Civil War lot will be put to auction on September 16."

"Oh, and ma'am," Merle said, "lemme ask you one more question: Is there a real fine Civil War pistol included with that lot?"

"Yes sir, it's the signature piece of the collection."

Once again, Merle was set back on his heels. "Did Al lie to us, Viv? Said he was donating, but instead he's selling? This doesn't seem right; sure doesn't look good."

Viv was peeling potatoes for potato salad. "When we saw him at Maybelle's 'going away party'…" She burst out laughing. "Sorry, I'm still seein' Charlene Cleland in her Pepto-Bismol pink T-shirt and Sheriff Judd… rollin' on the floor!" She dried her hands as Candy and the baby emerged from the bedroom.

Candy handed Maddy to Viv who held the baby at arm's length. "Baby Maddy, there's some real funny people lives here in Fruitvale! Yes, there are!" The baby smiled and giggled and even Merle had to laugh out loud. Candy smiled, seemed more engaged, listened closely to the conversation.

"As I was saying," Viv continued, "Alvin seemed so honest about donating the papers and all to the museum. Unless, he wanted us to think that…"

A perplexed look darkened Merle's genial face. He continued thinking. Squeezed into the tight space at Candy's computer, he turned his big body sideways and asked himself more questions: *How come it's taking so long to get Maybelle's time of death? Where's Soon Ha? Who killed Jimmy Chung and why? Why'd I receive a threatening note in Korean? Was Sheriff Judd at the Korean barbecue restaurant on official business—in the middle of the night? Who were the guys who followed me? Was the sheriff at Maybelle's the night she died? What's the Korean connection? Did Alvin Clegg kill his aunt?*

Candy interrupted his thoughts. "Honey, you had a good conversation with that lady district attorney. Why don't you try talking with her some more?"

"Just what I was fixin' to do, sweetie." Merle dialed and asked to speak to Tanequa Milwood. She answered straightaway.

"Afternoon, ma'am," he said. "I want to thank you for keeping the agent on watch outside our house here. Comforts us; we've all been real nervous since I got the crazy note in Korean."

"I'm so sorry, Merle, that your family has had to worry. I can tell you arrests will be forthcoming, and you'll be reassured when that happens."

Merle asked a careful question. "Can you tell me anything more about that? Especially about Jimmy Chung's death?"

"All I can say is that the SBI and the FBI are all over it."

"The FBI?"

"Some charges will be made soon. Be patient, Merle."

"Yes, ma'am, and since I'm bothering you anyway, lemme ask you a bunch more questions. Sheriff Judd has filed charges against Seth and his mom. We talked about how Seth was at the house way after Ms. Jordan was murdered. Do they have the time she was killed, actual time she died? That'll prove my buddy Seth isn't the killer."

"We're re-examining the details of Maybelle Jordan's murder. Can't say more than that."

"Okay, well, thanks ma'am. I know you're real busy right now."

"I'll keep you informed, Merle. I must go… but I assure you arrests will be made soon and will ease your worries about the threat to your family. Be patient, Merle."

Merle clicked off the phone and shook his head. "Sweetie, Granny Viv, I hate all this—people getting murdered, people being threatened, being hateful. What's happenin'? Ever'body used to be respectful, never wanted to hurt nobody, helped one another, cared about each other's kids and family as much as their own. I can't stand all this bad stuff."

"Things change, Merle. What you're talkin' about are 'small-town values.' I think they're still here… look around at your neighbors, your work buddies… if you or Candy needed something they'd be right here to help."

"Guess you're right, Viv. Bad stuff happens ever'where. Guess, right now it's Fruitvale's time for the bad stuff to happen."

Merle extracted himself from behind Candy's computer and headed to the fridge. He zoned in on a chunk of peach pie. His mind racing, he grabbed a fork and shoveled big bites of pie into his mouth. "Need a real sit-down with the DA," he mumbled.

Candy tipped her head at Merle and gave him a dark look as if to say, "Too many calories, too much sugar, Merle…" But she said nothing. She'd work on his health and diet later.

They'd all wait until the dust settled.

CHAPTER 20

"MS. MILWOOD, I SURE HOPE I'm not taking up your time for no good reason. Know you're real busy," Merle said. "But I learned a couple of things might be important." He waited for the district attorney to take her seat then he squeezed into a chair across from her.

Tanequa Milwood drew up a legal pad and uncapped a pen. "No problem, Merle, what are your concerns?"

"Has to do with Alvin Clegg, that's Ms. Maybelle Jordan's nephew…"

"Yes, Sheriff Judd contacted him after the murder."

"Well, hope I can explain this so it makes sense: Alvin told ever'body he's donating an important—probably valuable—collection of Civil War stuff—that his Aunt Maybelle had—to a museum. Stuff's been in the family long-time; he wanted it in a museum to honor-like his Aunt Maybelle."

"And…"

"Turns out, he didn't donate it—selling it at auction. Right up front, that kinda says he's tryin' to make some money off the stuff rather than donating like he said he would. Also, neighbor across the street from Ms. Jordan—her name is Edna Edgebert— told me that Ms. Jordan treated Alvin Clegg awful, called him names, did not approve of him, that sorta thing."

"Are you saying Alvin Clegg had motive to kill his aunt?"

"Hard for me to believe Al would murder anybody, but maybe she just pushed him off the edge."

"All very interesting, I may have a talk with Alvin Clegg."

"Do you mean have a talk with him or do you mean you'll question him as a suspect in Maybelle's murder?"

Tanequa Milwood answered carefully. "It would be unofficial. We're merely sorting out facts, clearing up unanswered questions."

Merle hesitated. "Uh, ma'am, would Sheriff Judd sit in at that meeting?"

The district attorney looked down at her note pad. "I'll inform him if there's anything of substance."

"Ma'am, I know this is not how you do things, but I'd sure like to sit in on that conversation with Al. I know him from school days and all, and I don't think he'd mind explaining some stuff if I'm there. I talked to him before about his aunt and all."

"That would be highly unusual, Merle." She thought for a moment, "Maybe it would put him at ease, so he can explain his decision to sell the collection rather than donate it. It would cleanse suspicion about his aunt's death. Tell you what, Merle, I'll arrange for a meeting in my office. Maybe in a day or two—I've a lot on my plate right now, but I'll get to a discussion with Mr. Clegg. I'll have my assistant call you when we have it arranged."

"Yes, ma'am, I'm available when you need me."

"You'll hear from me, Merle. Thanks for coming in today."

CHAPTER 21

MERLE PARKED THE PICKUP BEHIND the Fruitvale Redeemer Baptist Church which also was home to the local Korean Baptist Church. He sat for a moment reflecting on the death of a good person, Jimmy Chung. Merle's heart ached. "I'll never see Jimmy again," he grieved. "I liked that man so much. Things will never be the same…"

He set aside his sad thoughts and entered the church for an appointment with Reverend Cho, minister of the Korean Baptist church. He found Reverend Cho in his office. They shook hands.

"What can I do for you, Merle?" Reverend Cho asked.

"Need your advice, sir," Merle began. "Need to know if there are Korean customs or traditions we should observe when we visit the Chung family. We regular ol' Baptists just have a wake, then a regular funeral service. What do you have planned for the Chung family?"

"That's very kind and considerate of the family," Reverend Cho said. "The Chungs have been here for a long time. When I discussed this with Marie and her father-in-law, they expressed their desire for the event to be more American than Korean. By that I mean, they'll observe their own family and Korean traditions, but they don't expect their friends in the community to do anything other than what they ordinarily would do. So, Merle, just do what your instincts tell you."

"So, we should just go visit, then go to the funeral service?

Candy's mom wondered if it's okay to bring food, like she would for other family or friends."

"Of course, Merle. Tell her to make whatever gestures of sympathy—whether American or Korean—all will be greatly appreciated."

"We'll do that, Reverend," Merle said. "Thank you, sir." He turned to leave then asked, "Reverend Cho, why do things like this happen? Why does a really good person like Jimmy Chung, who only tried to do the right thing…" Merle was overcome, near tears, could not continue. Reverend Cho, who was nearly half Merle's height, looked up at him and said, "We will never know or understand, Merle. When tragedy strikes, we are surely tested. The important thing is how we come together and comfort one another." He extended his hand. "And your coming here today to see to comfort of the Chung family—well, you've passed the test."

Merle, unable to speak, nodded and shook Reverend Cho's hand.

At home, he told Viv and Candy, "Reverend Cho says the Chung family'll have a regular kind of wake, Baptist kind of funeral—but they'll do their own family traditions for themselves. He said we can bring food and visit like we would anyone else who's lost family."

"The wake should be underway at the Chungs. We must go and show Marie and family how much we care," Viv said quietly. "Lemme wrap up this big ham and potato salad." Candy removed a giant pan of brownies from the oven. "Soon as these cool and Ms. Green next door comes over to babysit Maddy, we'll be ready to go," she said.

Viv and Candy, each wearing a neat black dress, were dressed for the occasion. They waited for Merle to change clothes, to get into his wedding and funeral suit. Once again, he struggled to button the tight garment, did his best.

They arrived at the home of the Chung family, and the small house was filled with people. The first thing Merle, Candy, and Viv noticed was a large framed picture of Jimmy resting on the mantle of the fireplace. The portrait was of a younger Jimmy when he served in the U.S. Air Force. He wore the blue uniform well, his captain's bars visible at the shoulders, a number of bars on his chest showing various honors. Beneath the mantle, the fireplace was banked with layers of flowers, mostly white chrysanthemums.

Merle whispered, "I knew he was in the Air Force, didn't know he was a captain."

When Candy glimpsed the picture, she caught her breath and nearly cried out. Merle held her around the waist. "We gotta be strong for Marie," he whispered, his own eyes filling with tears. They found Marie and her mother sitting in the small dining room. They approached her with "I'm so sorry; he was such a good man; we'll miss him so much." Marie thanked them for coming, and speaking Korean to her mother explained that they were very special friends indeed. Her mother smiled a sad smile and nodded. They turned to Jimmy's father who stood and hugged each of them. He held on to Merle for a rather long time—the two making an odd pair—one very tall and the other diminutive. Mr. Chung pushed away and held Merle by his arms. "Jimmy like you best, Merle. He admire you. Said you are honest man. Man who helps others. He like you very best."

Merle could barely speak. "Jimmy—was an honest man—who helped others, Mr. Chung. He knew what was right."

The next day, the funeral for Jimmy Chung was held at the Fruitvale Baptist Church. The two ministers, the Very Reverend Cho and Reverend Jedforth officiated. The service alternated in two languages. The full choir sang.

Viv pronounced it, "The saddest funeral I've ever been to."

CHAPTER 22

Edna Edgebert stood at her front window—her last appraisal of the day—to view and to assess the coming and goings of her neighbors. As always, her disapproving scowl reflected her general disapproval of the world in general; but at this time of night, her censuring visage was slathered with a thick layer of moisturizer. Her hair was wrapped up in a multi-colored turban, her plump body clad in her cozy robe and her feet shod in bunny slippers. As she reached up to draw thick drapes closed, she glimpsed low-beam headlights slowly approaching from down the street. She watched the unfamiliar car come to a stop a few houses away. "Who could that be?"

A figure exited the auto and hurried up the walk. She recognized the gait, the body type. "For heaven's sake, that's…"

To her amazement, the figure turned and climbed her front steps. "What's he up to?" she wondered out loud.

A loud knock shook the door. "What the hell you want this time of night?" she called out.

"Need to talk to you, Edna. Open the door, please."

She opened the door. "What you need? It's damn near midnight!"

Her visitor stared at her—silent, menacing, scowling. Without warning, he shoved her into the living room, yanked the door closed, and leaned his back against it. He wore dark clothing, a nondescript zippered jacket, black pants. A dark ball cap pulled so far down over his forehead, he had to tilt his head up to look at her.

Edna stood her ground. "What the hell you doin' pushing your way into my home? Explain yourself or get the hell out!"

He did not answer. He stepped forward and with both hands shoved her down,

knocking over a dry, half-dead potted plant and causing a table lamp to crash to the floor. She lay sprawled, a look of terror screamed through the face cream. She cried out, "What…?"

He dropped forward and pressed his knees into her torso. Her arms and legs flailed, unable to grab or to push him away. His left hand pushed down her head, and his right slapped away her thrashing arms. He transferred one knee to her chest. She tried to yell; no breath or sound would flow. His weight held her pressed to the floor.

Calmly, silently, his gloved hands moved to her neck and choked the life out of her.

CHAPTER 23

GRANNY VIV ARRIVED EARLY AND began preparing breakfast for the family. Candy tended to the baby while Viv slapped together biscuits, bacon, scrambled eggs. The smell of a good breakfast filled the doublewide.

Candy leaned down and placed Maddy in her playpen. She handed her a rubber teething ring. "Those toothies comin' in, sweet girl?" Maddy giggled and promptly placed the baby toy in her mouth.

Candy reached for the remote and clicked on the television. The volume was low, so only she heard the alarming news. She clutched her heart and yelled, "Oh my, oh my," she repeated. "Oh, my! Merle come here—quick!"

Merle came out of the bathroom, having shaved, a towel at his face. He stared at the television. "No, not another one," he breathed out.

Candy upped the volume. A news anchor with perfect makeup and wearing a dress more suitable for cocktails than a morning newscast asked this question: "Is there a serial killer loose in Fremont County? The latest victim is Edna Edgebert, neighbor of Maybelle Jordan who was murdered about two and half weeks ago. A suspect in the Jordan murder is in jail and charged. Today Sheriff Judd and his team have another murder to investigate."

Merle sank to the edge of the sofa, causing it to make a

thunking sound. "Why is this happening? Why would someone kill that lady?" Agitated, Merle raised his big frame and turned away. "This is making me sick to my stomach. So awful. People murdered, a good man like Jimmy Chung, my good friend Seth in jail, what else can happen?"

At that moment, the newscaster announced, "In other news, District Attorney Tanequa Milwood will have a news conference at 9 a.m. The State Bureau of Investigation, the Federal Bureau of Investigation, and Drug Enforcement Agency will also be making statements regarding local illegal drug activity and recent arrests. Stay with us; we'll be going to that news conference in just a few…"

Merle sighed loudly. "At least they caught some bad guys. Wonder who they are." He sat, this time easing down carefully as to not damage the sofa. He could not relax, rose again, and paced the floor until time for the news conference.

Finally, Tanequa Milwood stood at a podium with a large group behind her. "Good morning," she said. "Today, with the assistance of law enforcement from the State Bureau of Investigation, the FBI, and the DEA, we have arrested Dae-Ho Kim and Kwang-Sun Kim, owners of the Joh Suh restaurant. The charges against the Misters Kim are serious. They are accused of murdering Jimmy Chung, well-known business owner in Fruitvale. Mr. Chung was an informant, a trusted member of our investigative team, who gathered important information about the Kim brothers who were receiving and dispensing illegal drugs, stolen goods, and laundering money. Both men are in jail as I speak. They have numerous serious charges against them, the most serious is, of course, the murder of Jimmy Chung."

Astounded, Merle looked around at Viv and Candy.

Both stood frozen, wide-eyed, their hands over their mouths. Recovering her voice, Candy whispered, "Jimmy Chung was working for the police? An 'informant?' Who would have guessed this?"

Merle moaned, "Here he was doing the right thing… what a terrible price he paid for saving our community from those bad guys." Merle crossed his arms over his wide body and hugged and rocked himself. "Jimmy Chung, Jimmy Chung…"

Tanequa Milwood continued, "We have arrested two other men, both Korean nationals in the U.S. illegally, who served as look-outs and "enforcers" for the Kim brothers. They are in Fremont County jail awaiting investigation by Immigration agents."

A thought struck Merle: *Had to be the guys who followed me home that night from the barbecue joint.* He kept this thought to himself… no reason to alarm Viv or to have to explain why he was out in the middle of the night.

Merle listened to the other charges outlined by the district attorney. He gasped in amazement when he recognized Karina Evans standing behind her. "Now, I'd like to introduce Karina Evans," Tanequa Milwood said. "Ms. Evans is the agent-in-charge for the investigation of the Kim brothers and their illegal activities."

Karina Evans approached the podium. Merle was incredulous. "An' I thought she was just the wife of a professor," he said out loud.

"Guess that's just her wife job," Viv said. "Other job's getting criminals."

Merle and Viv listened to other law enforcement professionals, including Agent Rodney Taylor of the SBI whom Merle had met the day he found Maybelle's body. He explained the Korean restaurant was integral to the distribution of illegal drugs in

Fremont County. The Kim brothers had ties to organized crime and criminal activity centered in Koreatown in Los Angeles.

The television camera panned the sizable group assembled for the news conference. Merle spied Sheriff Delbert Judd at the far-left side—looking rather out of place and uncomfortable. The sheriff shifted his weight and frequently crossed and uncrossed his arms. At times, he looked unsteady, seemed to wobble.

Merle kept thinking about his nighttime visit to the restaurant, his glimpse of the Korean brothers and someone else who looked very familiar. "Need to talk with Ms. Milwood again," he thought. "This is something else, altogether."

Viv opened the front door of the doublewide and peered out. "SBI agent's gone, Merle." She closed the door and leaned her back against it. "We don't have to worry so much."

Merle sighed relief. "Yep, all's good. Maybe I can go back to work, get out there with the mowin' crew."

"I'm so grateful they captured the evil people who killed nice Jimmy Chung. Jimmy Chung who was just trying to the right thing," Candy said, sadly. "I guess that's one down, two to go… now, who killed Maybelle Jordan and who killed Edna Edgebert?"

Viv headed back to her breakfast making. "I so hope it's not Alvin Clegg."

CHAPTER 24

THE NEXT DAY, MERLE DEVOURED the local paper and the news of the big drug bust and the apprehension of the thugs responsible for Jimmy's death. "Relief to know the Kim brothers are in jail, and they'll pay for what they did to Jimmy." He sighed. "Just doesn't bring back a good man like Jimmy."

He folded the paper and looked down at the breakfast Candy had prepared for him. Oatmeal with raisins, whole-wheat toast (the butter absent), and a plate of sliced apples and pears. "Candy, this looks like a 'healthy' breakfast for sure." He gave her his sad sack glance.

"Yesterday, honey, you ate four of Granny Viv's biscuits with butter and peach jam. Today—not so many calories and fat— have to pay the price today for what you bought yesterday."

"Yes, ma'am," he said. He saluted. "Private Merle Hucken followin' orders, Colonel Candy."

Candy smiled. "I'm not your drill instructor, Merle. I'm your wife, and I care about your health. We're just making some life-style changes to stay healthy."

"Yes, ma'am!" He ate the oatmeal slowly and pretended it was "loaded hash browns," the specialty of the local Fruitvale breakfast place, Early's Grill—hash browns, sausage, bacon, and fried eggs topped with sour cream and hot sauce—all filling a wide plate. The oatmeal, somehow, was not quite the same, but he knew better than to complain.

As he was finishing breakfast, his cell rang. "Mornin', sir… Yes sir, 'course I remember you, Agent Taylor. Met you when we found Ms. Jordan's body out there off the highway… you want me to… do what now? Okay, I'll come talk with you, be there in a few minutes."

"Now, what? What you got goin' this morning?" Candy asked as she set Maddy in the high chair and prepared to open a jar of baby food.

"That was Rodney Taylor with the SBI. Said Ms. Milwood's tied up with all this Korean stuff, and she wants me to talk with Agent Taylor about Alvin Clegg…"

Merle drew his battered pickup into the parking lot at Hardee's. Nervous and uncertain of his new role, he fingered the wire under his shirt. It extended to a recorder that was held in a holster-type contraption. "How'd I get myself into this," he asked himself. "Now I'm wearing a wire and investigating Alvin Clegg. I'm just a guy who mows, for crying out loud." While working at calming himself, Alvin Clegg's classy car pulled up next to him. He waved at Alvin who waved back.

Alvin greeted Merle with a handshake. "Good to see you, Merle. Nice to get together with you again."

"Well, me, my wife Candy, and her mom Viv keep wondering about you—how you're doin' since Ms. Jordan's death. I told them I'd buy you coffee and check up on you."

"That's very kind of, Merle, but coffee's on me. What's your pleasure?"

"Hey, this was my invitation!"

Alvin Clegg raised his hand and tipped his head as if to say, "I'm buying."

Merle acquiesced. "Okay. Regular old joe. Thanks, Al. I'll grab us a table."

Alvin brought two steaming coffees to the table. Merle shook two sugar packets, put one back, and stirred the contents of the other into his cup. "So, tell me how you're doin' so I can file my report with my ladies at home," Merle said.

"Well, I still don't know what's going on with the investigation into Aunt May's death. Wish they'd wrap that up. I know you're certain your buddy Seth isn't the culprit. Big question: who is?"

"Al, I would stake my life on it. Seth did not murder your aunt. I'm real afraid Sheriff Judd thinks he's got himself a slam-dunk."

"I understand Seth was at the house… that he moved the body out there where you guys found her."

"Correct, but your Aunt Maybelle was dead when he arrived at her house."

Alvin Clegg took blew steam from his coffee. "How do we know that?"

Merle walked Alvin through the scenario of Seth's arrival, removal of the body, and departure to place it where the two of them would find her later. As Merle told the details, he observed Alvin's reaction—surprise, great interest.

"Lemme ask you a question, Al," Merle said. "Has the Civil War stuff been set up at the museum? Candy and Viv would like to go there and see it sometime."

"Oh, there's a change in plans. I decided to sell the collection through Luthely's in Greenville. I really agonized about the decision, especially after I announced it would go to the museum."

"Why the change of plans?"

"You remember Mr. Jenkins, our history teacher in high school? He's retired now, but he volunteers in the school library. Had a long talk with him, and he suggested money from sale of the collection could improve the school library with new technology. There is literally no way for the kids to do on-line research and such. I think it would be better use of the money for an immediate need, and who knows? Whoever buys the collection will eventually donate it to a museum. Does that make sense?"

Merle nodded, uncertain what to ask next.

"And there's more to the story, Merle. It's kind of personal, but I think I can tell you. Aunt May did not approve of me. Didn't like who I am—called me 'sissy;' said I wasn't a 'real man.'" Alvin's gray eyes filled with tears; he twisted his diamond ring nervously then took a quick gulp of coffee.

"Hey, I'm listening," Merle said. "I had no idea. Musta been tough on you."

Alvin blurted, "She once told me to buy me girls' underwear, that's how 'sissified' I was." He shifted in the seat and seemed angry. "Merle, all the stuff I endured from her—she refused to speak to me for years because of my relationship with a man." He took deep breaths as if trying to get control of his emotions. "Isn't it interesting? She had a moral bias against my lifestyle, while hers was—well, you know how she supported herself. Meanwhile, I'm in a loving monogamous relationship, and she had her "boyfriends" as she called them."

Merle did not know what to say, but finally breathed out, "Did she ever change her way of thinking? Was she more understanding, I mean—did she ever show she had changed?"

Alvin swallowed hard and took a moment to answer. "Yes, she did. I told her I was in a relationship with a wonderful person, and I think she began paying more attention to the news about gay marriage and gay rights, and somehow she came around."

Merle hardly knew what to say. "Hey, that was a good thing…" he said at last.

"She asked me to dinner a few months ago and actually apologized. Said she was very sorry she'd been so mean." He looked down at his coffee. "But you know, Merle, I had so many years of pain and heartache from her—disposing of the Civil War memorabilia is a way to put it all behind me. I said I was going to donate the collection. But it has so many bad memories for me, I just wanted to give it to someone else. Someone I don't know who will take it and put it somewhere—out of sight, out of mind—so to speak. I'll see the money goes to worthy causes. Maybe it'll make some of the pain go away, heal my feelings made so raw by Aunt May's criticism."

Merle sat quietly, his big hands encircling his coffee cup. Finally, he said, "Think that makes a lot of sense, Al. Do some good with the money from the sale." He swirled the last of his coffee and took a sip. "Whole thing's painful, for sure. Sorry you had to go through all that. And then having her die the way she did, you've had a rough time."

Alvin didn't answer, blinked away tears.

Merle broke the silence. "Curious. When was the last time you talked with your aunt before she died?"

"Night before. I took the last boxes of the collection from her house. She was actually really pleasant to me that evening, now that I think about it. At least, I didn't have to hear the abusive stuff she could come up with..." He looked away. "Maybe that's a good way to remember her."

"Did you ever find the pistol?"

"Yes, as a matter of fact. It was at the back of a drawer in Aunt May's bureau. I completely missed it when I gathered things earlier."

Tanequa Milwood, dressed in a slim-fitted red suit, greeted Merle with a handshake. "Rod Taylor and I listened to your conversation with Alvin Clegg. How do you think it went, Merle?"

Although her attire livened up her complexion and looked very chic, her wan expression and tired brown eyes reflected late hours poring over a small mountain of work.

"I sure was uncomfortable wearing the wire. Kept askin' myself what the heck I was doing, but at least it all eased my mind about Alvin Clegg. Ma'am, I don't think Alvin Clegg murdered his aunt," Merle said. He wedged himself into the chair across her as she turned to sit behind her desk.

The district attorney leaned her elbows forward on the desk and clasped her hands in front of her. "Neither do I," she said.

"I'm real embarrassed. I caused you lots of extra trouble. Sorry for this whole wild goose chase, ma'am."

"Criminal investigation can have lots of wild goose chases, Merle. Process of elimination and all that. We go down a lot of wrong roads before we find the right one." She tipped her head and looked at Merle for a long moment. "No one, Merle—other than you—could have posed the right questions to Mr. Clegg. Your participation was worth it to eliminate him as a suspect."

Merle, his mind racing, decided to go for the most unlikely theory of all: "Ma'am, I drove to the Korean restaurant back before Jimmy Chung was killed, before you arrested the Kim brothers. It was late at night, and I will swear I saw Sheriff Delbert Judd with them. Now, there could be lotsa reasons why he'd talk to them, but why at one a.m. in the early morning?"

"Go on, Merle. Tell me what you're thinking." Tanequa pulled forward her legal pad and jotted a line of notes.

"Ms. Edgebert, the neighbor across from Ms. Jordan, said the sheriff visited there every Wednesday night. Heard another lady who showed up at Ms. Jordan's funeral confirm the sheriff was her 'Wednesday night guy.'"

"And Maybelle Jordan was killed in the early hours of Thursday morning…"

"Now, ma'am, I'm not saying Sheriff Judd is the murderer,

but it seems like he would divulge that he was at the woman's house very close to the time of her death. Wouldn't that be important for him to reveal so there's no suspicion on him?"

Tanequa Milwood took time to answer, drew lines and circles on her legal pad. She did not lift her head or look directly at Merle. "I believe Sheriff Judd is still investigating."

Merle felt he'd said all he could. He extracted himself from the small office chair and stood. "I know you're real busy, ma'am, so I'll make myself scarce. I hope I helped showing Alvin Clegg did not have anything to do with Ms. Jordan's murder. If there's anything else, I can…"

Tanequa raised a finger as if to say, "As a matter of fact…" She stood and walked around to the front of the desk, folded her arms, and stared directly at Merle.

"Merle, would you be willing to wear that wire again?"

CHAPTER 25

"SHERIFF DELBERT JUDD'S OFFICE. DEPUTY Clarke, speaking. How may I help you?"

"Morning, sir, this is Merle Hucken calling for Sheriff Judd. Like to speak with him, please."

"Sheriff's out of the office. Is this an emergency?"

"No, sir, not an emergency, but I would like to have a talk with him. Know when he'll be back? I can call then."

"I'll take a message and have him return your call."

"I appreciate it. Please tell him Merle Hucken called, and I'd like to make an appointment for a sit-down conversation with him as soon as convenient. Here's my number…"

"Got it. I'll see he gets the message."

"Many thanks. Appreciate it."

Merle clicked off the phone and congratulated his calmness. *Guess I can hold it together to do this… how'd I get into this? My best friend's in jail, I been threatened by the Korean mafia… who woulda thought a guy like me…?*

That evening, Merle reached for his cell phone to hear the clipped voice of Sheriff Delbert Judd. "What you want, boy? Don't be callin' me none unless you got some real information for my investigation. I'm a busy man!"

"Yes, sir, you have a lot goin' on. I just wondered if maybe we could meet for a cup of coffee; I'd like to explore the time sequence of when my buddy Seth was at the crime scene, and review a few things regarding the facts of the case." Merle took a deep breath and could not believe he'd just used phrases like "explore the time sequence" and "regarding the facts of the case."

"You still think you're some kind of detective, don't ya, Merle Hucken?"

"No sir, I am not a detective, but I do think it's important to review the facts that you determined were sufficient to charge Seth Wilkins with murder. There is more to the case, and I believe it's important you consider additional facts. I agree, you are a very busy man, so you may not have had an opportunity to explore these facts—to the full extent." Merle held the phone away from his ear to catch his breath, unbelieving that it was he who was speaking this way. He wondered if his huge body had been occupied by someone other than the good ol' boy who mows.

Merle could hear the sheriff's phlegm-rattling breathing. "Okay, boy, you come on over my office tomorrow morning. Eleven a.m. An' you better have something worthy to say and not waste my time none."

"Thank you, sir. I'll be there at eleven, and it will not be a waste of your time." Merle clicked off the phone and held it to his pounding heart. "What the heck am I doin'?"

The next morning, Merle checked phone messages. A message from Sheriff Judd: "too busy to meet you this mornin,' meet me tonight at Marker 45 on Highway 36, where you discovered the remains of Ms. Maybelle Jordan. We can review the facts at that scene. I got me a real busy day, so won't get there until late—nine, nine-thirty."

At nine p.m. on the dot, Merle's old pickup clunked to a stop at Marker 45 on Highway 36. Nervous and perspiring, he killed the engine but kept the headlights burning. He fingered the wire, pulled at the police vest he wore under an old sweatshirt. The vest, the largest they had, fit oddly, causing his thin T-shirt underneath to bunch up. Edges of the vest itched and chafed against his skin. He tugged at the layers of fabric, but the vest and T-shirt rode high and stuck to his clammy belly. The well-washed sweatshirt seemed a good camouflage and comfort choice for the occasion; but the night was warm and humid.

Merle was physically uncomfortable and emotionally uncomfortable as well. The bad memory of finding Maybelle Jordan, the gruesome condition of her body, the shock of it, came flooding back. He felt sick again. *I gotta get over this. Too much on the line, right now. Gotta get this right for Ms. Milwood and Agent Taylor and, most of all, for Seth.*

He waited for what seemed hours but was, more than likely, less than twenty minutes. A nondescript sedan drew up from the opposite side of the road, and the lights dimmed. Sheriff Judd held open the car door and heaved his bulbous body up and out. He headed toward Merle and ordered, "Boy, you come on over by this short stand o' trees. We'll have us our talk here."

Merle stood from the pickup and leaned the door shut. He pulled in his stomach and straightened his shoulders, telling himself to "keep cool, keep calm."

"Yes, sir," he called out and walked slowly to where the sheriff stood. "Not sure why we're way out here. We coulda talked in your office or over coffee at Hardee's. Know we're out where I tripped over poor Ms. Jordan, but there's no more to tell about that."

The sheriff snorted his usual bluster. "And so what's there to tell we can't talk 'bout out here?"

Merle did not answer, struggled to formulate his thoughts. Darkness had descended; dim moonlight and the headlights of Merle's old pickup did a poor job illuminating the area where the sheriff was heading. "Tell you what, sir, got me a flashlight back here in my truck. Kinda dark now." Before the sheriff could object, he hurried to the pickup, reached in, and pulled out a large flashlight—the one he carried when on duty as a volunteer firefighter. Clicking it on, his shoulders pulled back and his body tense, he strode toward the sheriff.

"Just don't aim that damn thing at my eyes. Follow me on over this way," the sheriff ordered. "Wanna tell you a couple things over here."

Merle followed, seemingly obedient, but his mind raced, his heart thudded. Dripping perspiration, nauseous and sick as the day he tripped over Maybelle Jordan, he felt as if operating on some sort of automatic pilot. His feet moved as if someone else were directing them. He dogged the sheriff—kicking aside fallen branches and stumbling over rocks. Finally, the sheriff pushed through low branches into an open area. They were well away from the highway.

Hazy moonlight poked through the overcast sky from time to time, aiding Merle's flashlight to cut the darkness. He scanned the area with his flashlight. Perhaps they were in the clearing where they'd found Maybelle's body; he could not be certain. He directed the flashlight at the sheriff's midsection, away from his eyes. He spoke in a clear, calm voice, "Yes, Sheriff Judd, I believe this is where we found Ms. Jordan, but we all know she was killed at her home. We also know the real facts, sir, that Seth found her dead at her home. We know he made a stupid mistake by moving the body and placing it way out here. Seth Wilkins is innocent."

"Look, fat boy, I'm not goin' over and over this again with you. I told you and told you to back off, to get outta my way, outta the way of my investigation. But no, you don't listen good, do you?"

Suddenly calmer, Merle aimed the flashlight beam up at the

sheriff's torso. The light followed the sheriff's gloved hand as it moved to his hip, to the handle of his revolver.

The sheriff spat out words. "Git used to it, boy. Your buddy Seth Wilkins is goin' up the creek for the murder of Maybelle Jordan."

"Sir, I'll say it for the hundredth time, Seth did not kill the woman. He's only guilty of moving the body."

"Well, aren't them interesting facts? And now, 'cuz of your meddlin', your in-ter-fer-ing, that skinny bitch DA is askin' too many questions, questioning my re-ports, my in-ves-ti-ga-tive de-tails."

"Is that 'cuz of me, Sheriff?" Merle called out, his voice steady and clear, though he was soaked with sweat and his heart pounded. "Or is it because you've been giving wrong details and trying to railroad my buddy Seth Wilkins?"

Merle sensed fury building in the already-angry sheriff. The sheriff tightened his grip on the gun handle.

Before he could answer, Merle called out again—he was shouting now, his voice more high-pitched than usual. "Come clean, Sheriff! Who really killed Maybelle Jordan?"

The sheriff threw back his head and choked out a phlegm-filled laugh. "How the hell do I know? But all intents and purposes, it's your boy Seth. It'll be clear and easy to convince a jury he was there and did the deed—to avenge his mama and family who hated Maybelle Jordan. Simple as that."

Merle, swaying somewhat as he processed the unethical information the sheriff had just spewed out, continued shining the light directly at the sheriff. The sheriff kept his hand on his gun; the other he held to his forehead to shade his eyes from the flashlight beam. There were soft sounds all around them—rustling, twigs snapping, branches moving. A louder sound, perhaps of a branch falling, drew the sheriff's attention. He turned his head. "What the hell's that?"

"Deer," Merle stated calmly. "Big deer herd out this way. See 'em when we mow and hack back over this far from the highway. Bunches of deer. Lots of fawns, this year."

The sheriff glanced from side to side; the moon had slipped behind clouds; the only light came from Merle's flashlight.

Merle, suddenly refocused and determined, yelled, "Why are you doing this to Seth? Why don't you investigate who really murdered Maybelle Jordan? You said you and she were long-time friends."

The sheriff pulled the gun from his hip and pointed it directly at Merle and the light glowing from his flashlight.

The sheriff tipped his head back, screwed up his chin, his mouth turned down. "'Cuz election's comin' up, an' I need a conviction to look good to my con-stit-u-ency. And 'sides, I got bigger problems than May's murder." The sheriff coughed, ran the back of his hand over his mouth. He re-aimed the gun and held it steady at the beam of Merle's flashlight.

Merle suppressed his rattled nerves and yelled, "Since it looks like you're gonna just blow me away with that gun of yours, tell me what these 'bigger problems' are…"

"Well now, that skinny bitch D.A.'s sniffin' 'round too much, that's what." He aimed the gun with both hands. "Know what, Merle Hucken, I'm gettin' real tired of your 'need to know.' What the hell else? We're gonna wrap this up."

"Did you not think," Merle asked in a calm, measured manner, "that you'd be a suspect? Because you were one of Maybelle Jordan's visitors?"

"For your in-for-ma-tion, fat boy, I was not there—at her place—the night she croaked."

"It's thought you were a regular at her house on Wednesday nights."

"Once in a while, May needs a break, I guess, 'cuz she called, said she had a cold—I s'pect she had some other guy on deck."

"Do you know who?"

"Oh, hell, there were so many men visited her, take a number. I dunno… all I know is your buddy Seth Wilkins made it real convenient to be the guy who did it. What a stupid ass, movin' a body."

Merle held his tongue, wanted to yell, "Not as stupid as sending an innocent man to jail for something he did not do." He collected his thoughts and asked, "So you're telling me you did not kill Maybelle Jordan, you don't know who did, and Seth just made it easy for you to look good to get elected."

"You are for sure one dumb sonovabitch, boy. Sure, I visit May on Wednesdays, but the night she was killed she had a cold and said not to come by. I was over at the Stags Lodge shootin' darts with the boys. Alibi's iron tight 'cuz there were a dozen other guys there. I beat old Lester Stebbins outta thirty dollars. Don't you think he'd remember that? Like I said, I didn't kill May. So, what else you gotta know?"

"What about Edna Edgebert?"

"What about the nosy bitch?"

"Who killed Edna Edgebert?" Merle's flashlight dimmed, flickered. He'd not thought to check the batteries.

"Prob-ly same yay-hoo who killed May. I dunno—wasn't me. Maybe your buddy Seth's mama 'cuz nosy Edna saw her boy carting May away. Hell, I dunno." He aimed the gun and steadied it with his other hand. "So boy, enough with the questions. Your questions are gonna be the end of you."

"Okay, okay," Merle breathed out. He raised his long arms, bending his right wrist, tipping the now-dim flashlight toward the sheriff. "I know I'm 'bout to join Maybelle and Edna, but I'd just like to know what you do with the Koreans." He kept his arms elevated. "Give a dying man one last bit of information. Might give me some peace o' mind when you pull that trigger."

Merle could not believe the clear and steady voice that came out of his own mouth. Again, he wondered if a new force—one calmer and stronger and wiser—now inhabited his huge, heavy-set body. "Why were you at the Korean barbecue joint with the Korean boys in the middle of the night? What'd you have goin' with them?"

The sheriff's voice took on a different tone, as if to explain to someone who didn't know much, who learned slowly. "Well, I'll tell you what, boy. You need to understand… sheriff's job's hard work, an' pay's not so great. A man's got to make a livin', an' when you like the finer things in life, you need cash. Now those Korean boys were my 'cash machine.' And they racked me up some good deposits that I could withdraw on a regular basis. All I had to do was look the other way while they ran their drugs, laundered their money. When that loser Jimmy Chung was double-dealing and rattin' them out, they got him outta the way."

"The Korean guys are charged with killing Jimmy Chung. You know for sure they're the murderers?"

"Boy, I am as-tound-ed as just how dumb you are. I just told you they 'got him outta the way.' What is it you don't understand when somebody says, 'got him outta the way'?"

"And Soon Ha? What happened to her?"

"Shipped her off to L.A., the mornin' you tripped over May's body."

"You questioned her?"

"Nah. Wrote up a report after she left saying she'd last seen May alive the day before."

By now, the sheriff's anger seemed to diminish, replaced by a hardened, determined attitude. "Okay, enough of this chit-chat. How you want this—in the back, chest, the head?

Not goin' for your fat belly. You got so much layerin' there, won't go that far in." The sheriff laughed, enjoying his own cruel joke.

Merle took deep breaths. Moving on his internal automatic

pilot, he tipped the now-faint flashlight glow directly at the sheriff's eyes. A shot rang out. Merle's heart stopped, but it was the sheriff who fell to the ground, clutching his thigh. He writhed on the ground, spewing a torrent of curse words.

A team of DEA agents and police surged forward, out from the trees, guns pointed at the sheriff's head.

Merle collapsed to the ground. Rodney Taylor, seemingly out of nowhere, rushed toward him. Pushing his night-vision goggles up on his forehead, he squatted down, placed his hand on Merle's shoulder. "You okay, Merle?" he asked.

Merle raised his head, to see the sheriff—now surrounded by law enforcement, illuminated by flashlights glowing from their helmets. The sheriff groaned, cursed Merle, Maybelle, Seth, Seth's mother, the DA, Rodney Taylor. As officers snapped cuffs on him and attended to his bleeding thigh, he sputtered. "Y'all go straight to hell!"

Merle collapsed back to the ground and breathed again.

Rodney Taylor extended his hand. "You've a brave man, Merle Hucken." He helped Merle to a sitting position; a young EMT rushed forward with a blood pressure cuff. Merle, shaking and dripping with sweat, slumped forward. Rodney and the EMT managed to pull the soaked sweatshirt off Merle. They unhooked the wire and unstrapped the vest, pulling it away from Merle's irritated skin. Rodney, the recorder/wire in hand, strode away to secure the devices. "Back in a bit, Merle. You sit tight; don't get up yet."

The EMT strapped the blood pressure cuff around Merle's wide bicep. "Take a deep breath, sir," he told Merle. "Try to relax. Your work's done, sir."

Looking up at the young man, Merle was so exhausted it took real effort to smile, to show gratitude.

"Whoa," the EMT breathed out, "210 over 100! Need to get calm, sir, relax now…"

Merle took deep breaths. "I... I..."

"No talking, sir, take it easy..."

After a while, they watched as the handcuffed sheriff, his swearwords and threats raging nonstop, was lifted on to a gurney. Two emergency workers strapped him down and elevated his injured leg. A tight wide compression bandage covered his thigh. The team lugged him forward, stepping over and around obstacles. They struggled with the heavy load, but managed to push through low branches and the stand of trees, to a waiting ambulance.

The EMT, squatting down by Merle, re-strapped the blood pressure cuff. "BP's comin' down, sir; just stay relaxed. Breath normally."

Merle looked up at the young man. "What's your name?"

"Darryl. Darryl Johnson."

"Hey, Darryl, nice to meet ya."

"It's honor to meet you, sir."

Merle chuckled slightly. "Nobody's ever said it's an 'honor.'"

"Is when the guy's a hero," Darryl replied.

Merle just shook his head. "You guys are the real heroes." He tried to relax. "How's the pressure now, Darryl?"

"Better." He looked up as Rodney Taylor approached. "I think we can get Mr. Hucken to a standing position now, sir." The two men heaved to help Merle move his now 300 pounds up to standing. His legs buckled, but he willed them to hold him vertical. "Just stand here now, sir. Let me check your standing BP."

Merle obeyed, but had to ask Agent Taylor, "Did everything get recorded?"

"Yes, Merle, we got the goods on ol' Sheriff Delbert Judd."

"But he didn't kill Maybelle Jordan or Edna Edgebert. We still don't know who did."

"We know more than we did, though, Merle—that Sheriff

Judd was protecting the Korean guys. We also know he didn't investigate the murder, that he was truly railroading Seth for political reasons."

Merle relaxed, and his blood pressure fell 60 points.

Merle arrived at home shortly after midnight; Candy and Viv met him at the door. Exhausted, he took each step up the porch slowly—one at a time. "Where were you?" Candy asked, "We were worried."

The phone rang; Candy returned inside to answer. Viv held the door open for the big man who looked as if he'd been dragged through the proverbial knothole. "Please tell us what's going on, Merle. We need to know what's goin' on!"

Once inside, a shocked Candy reported, "That was Agent Rodney Taylor. He says we have a returning hero, that Merle got important information, a confession from Sheriff Judd, and it's all recorded!" Viv's mouth fell open. "How'd you do that, Merle?" Candy asked.

Merle sat down heavily. "Important thing is," Merle whispered, his voice hoarse, "Seth won't be charged with murder. The sheriff made false statements, never investigated proper. Maybe the D.A. will find a way to get Seth outta jail… the sooner, the better."

Merle sighed and shook his head. "Still don't know who murdered those two ladies. There's still a murderer out there."

CHAPTER 26

T HE NEXT DAY, MERLE, CANDY, and Viv sat in the double-wide's small living area to watch the televised news of the sheriff's arrest. Tanequa Milwood, interviewed by a reporter, answered all questions in her professional and straightforward manner. As always, she appeared tired, stressed, but her voice was steady and businesslike. "Delbert Judd has been arrested for numerous serious crimes—aiding and abetting drug traf-ficking, money laundering, and falsifying evidence in a murder investigation. His confessions to all crimes are documented and will be presented as evidence to a grand jury as of Monday. In the meantime, Delbert Judd is in Fremont County jail awaiting charges. He is held without bond. He has legal representation and has been advised of his rights."

The reporters swarmed, yelled out questions, pressed for more details of the evidence and of the investigation. They probed how the sheriff was exposed. The district attorney raising her hands to gesture "enough," answered, "That is all I can tell you right now. When the charges are drawn up, I'll be holding a news conference and will answer all your questions."

A reporter called out, "What about Seth Wilkins? What's happened with his situation?"

"Seth Wilkins has not received due process of law," the D.A. said. "He will be released on bail. The murder investigation con-tinues. He faces a felony charge of tampering with a crime scene and failure to report a crime. I'll say no more as this remains an active investigation."

The reporters continued to press, call out questions. "News conference soon, everyone," the D.A. said. She turned and left.

Viv and Candy leapt from the chair. "Seth will be released," Candy shouted. Merle, although pleased, was subdued. "He's still not off the hook—not 'til the terrible guy who killed the two ladies is identified. I can't cheer until that happens."

Merle dialed his cell. "Ms. Wilkins, you heard the news?… Yes, ma'am, good news. When they release Seth, I'll come get you, and we'll go together to get him outta jail… first lemme talk to the DA's office and find out when they'll let him go… yes, ma'am, call you soon… you're welcome, Ms. Wilkins… yes, ma'am… me too, very happy… they'll find the killer… yes, ma'am."

CHAPTER 27

ERLE WAITED OUTSIDE THE DISTRICT Attorney's office. "Ms. Milwood will see you now, Mr. Hucken," her assistant said. "She's looking forward to talking with you."

"Thank you, ma'am." Merle entered Tanequa Milwood's office. As usual her office appeared that of a busy woman—the desk piled high with stacks of folders and documents, a credenza filled with more. She waited in front of her desk, dressed as always in a chic, slim suit, a wide smile on her face. "Well, if it isn't the hero of all Fremont County," she said as she extended her hand. "You have to feel good about your contribution to exposing the sheriff's nefarious dealings."

"Yes, ma'am! But we still don't have the killer, and my buddy Seth is not entirely off the hook, it seems to me."

"But we know more than we did because you were willing to wear the wire. Don't know who else could have done that for us and helped us so much."

"I did what I needed to do to help Seth. His mom is sure anxious to have him home. Can he be released soon? We'd like to come get him, get him home safe."

"Yes, I've scheduled his release for this afternoon. There are, as you well know, some charges filed against Seth…"

"Yes, ma'am, I do know that… and Seth knows that. And he has to post some kinda bail or bond?"

"Yes, and there are restrictions—such as—he cannot leave the county, must appear again in court on a designated date."

"Can he go back to work? I talked to our boss, and he said they'd let Seth come back to work if it's okay with you. I think that'd be the best thing for everyone concerned. Seth needs to get out there in the fresh air and do his work. And Seth's an honest man; he won't be taking off, not a risk."

"Yes, he can resume working, and I know he's not a flight risk, Merle," the DA said. "Tell Seth's mother that you and she can take Seth home this afternoon."

"And ma'am, I know you're busy, but could answer me a couple questions?"

"Of course, Merle, you've earned some answers. What do you want to know?"

"The 'time of death' detail—was that ever figured out, and did it show that Ms. Jordan was dead when Seth arrived at her house?"

Tanequa Milwood, turned her slim shoulders and walked to her desk chair. "Have a seat, Merle. This is going to take some time to lay out some facts." She gestured to the office chair in front of her desk. As always, Merle sat down carefully, wedging himself into the narrow seat.

"When you pointed out that Ms. Jordan was dead when Seth arrived, that he arrived at 6:30 a.m. and drove away at 6:40, that made me suspicious. Something was not right with the medical examiner's report. The document indicated time of death as 'approximately 5:45 a.m.' When I questioned Delbert Judd about the time of death, he became very defensive, was very rude. She laughed out loud. "He implied I was an 'uppity black girl who didn't know her place.'"

The D.A. looked pained. "Sorry, Merle, please forget I said that. That was unprofessional… let me just say, Delbert Judd did not alter the document nor could he have murdered Ms. Jordan—

he was at the Stags Lodge playing darts, was not visiting her that evening—even though, as I understand it, he was there nearly every Wednesday night. There are many at the Lodge who vouch for his whereabouts—and, one of the members escorted him home about 2:45 because he'd had a little too much to drink.

'I conferred with the medical examiner who was astounded that the death certificate had been tampered with. He ordered an independent review of the medical findings on Ms. Jordan."

Merle, fascinated with this information, leaned forward and asked, "So could they figure the time Ms. Jordan was really murdered?"

"Actual time of death was 1:30 a.m. At that exact time, Delbert Judd was at the Stags Lodge happily tossing darts and downing bourbon."

Merle paused. "Ma'am, this means there's still a murderer out there. Somebody who killed two women."

The DA nodded. "It's a chilling thought. Our investigation continues. At least we have the Kim brothers and a corrupt sheriff in custody. And thanks to you, Merle, the sheriff's guilt was confirmed on the recordings you managed to get during your confrontation out there off Highway 36. It's all admissible evidence against him. Feel sorry for his attorney; he'll be a hard one to defend, but I'm pretty sure former-sheriff Delbert Judd will spend his retirement years in Butner, North Carolina."

"Amen to that, Ms. Milwood. So, Seth can go home, go back to work, but there's still the murderer who's gotta get caught. I want for Seth to get his good name back. Know he made a terrible mistake, and he has to pay the price for that mistake… but he's a good man, just got caught up in something he let get out of control." Merle eased out of the tight chair and stood. "Well, Ms. Milwood, I'm gonna go get my buddy out of the hoosegow."

Tanequa Milwood stood and extended her hand. "Thank you,

Merle. Took a lot of courage to confront Delbert Judd out there in the woods."

"But I had a great team backin' me up, ma'am. They're the brave ones."

"Agreed. It takes a team of brave people to do what's needed. But thanks again for wearing the wire and asking all the right questions that night."

"Glad it turned out right… saved Seth from bein' railroaded for a murder he did not do." *But we won't rest easy until we know who killed Maybelle and her neighbor.*

Gotta keep asking questions.

CHAPTER 28

MERLE'S OLD PICKUP RATTLED UP to Pearl's home. He rang the bell. Pearl, dressed nicely, her hair done up, greeted him at the door with cigarette in hand. "Hey, Merle," she said. She stepped forward and holding the cigarette out and away from him, placed her other arm around him, and hugged him hard. Merle, taken off guard and cigarette smoke wafting in his face, said, "Ah, Ms. Wilkins, it's a good day we're getting Seth back."

Pearl stood back. She was crying. "Thanks, Merle, for believin' in my boy Seth."

"Yes, ma'am, you and I knew all along Seth wasn't guilty." He leaned down to Pearl, "Hey, dry those tears, we're happy now! Let's go get Seth-er!"

Pearl stubbed out her cigarette, dried tears, and blew her nose. She looked beyond the porch at Merle's sad old truck. She handed him car keys. "Let's take my SUV," she said.

Merle inserted himself into the driver's side of Pearl's car. As he fumbled to release the seat and make room for his long legs, Pearl pulled out her pack of Marlboros, glanced at Merle, and put the cigarettes back in her purse. "Trying to not smoke so much, Merle. Seth doesn't like it. I'm gonna try to be more considerate of him."

"Good for you, Ms. Wilkins. He'll appreciate that."

"An', Merle, I've learned my lesson. I was real hard on Seth about dating ladies not of our kind. That was wrong. I been givin' it a lot of thought. Whoever Seth chooses to love, well, that's his choice, not mine. I've been very wrong tryin' to change who he cares about. I was very wrong." Tearful, her voice caught. "I'm not gonna do that to him anymore."

Merle hardly knew what to say. "Seth's a smart man, Ms. Wilkins. Good that you give him credit for making his own choices. That's good, very good."

"I'm gonna tell him that whoever he chooses to love, it's okay, I'll learn to love her, too." Pearl Wilkins remained silent until they arrived at the jail. They waited while documents charging Seth with felony tampering of evidence and failing to report a homicide were drawn up. At last, a deputy escorted Seth out into the reception area. Merle was shocked at how thin and gaunt he'd become. His usually tanned and smooth skin was ashen; his clothing hung loose. He spied Merle and Pearl and headed toward them. Pearl jumped up and grabbed him around the waist and held on.

With his mother attached to him, he extended his hand to his old buddy. His eyes said, "I'm grateful, Merle. Thank you."

In the car, Seth said little. "How's my boy?" Pearl kept asking.

"Fine, Ma. I'm fine."

When they arrived at Pearl's and exited the car, Merle decided to forge ahead with suggestions. "Called our boss. Asked him if you could come back to work. Jorge said yes, no problem… sooner the better. Whadya think, Seth-er?"

Seth smiled a weary smile. "That sounds good. Is tomorrow too soon?"

Merle laughed his high-pitched laugh and gently slapped Seth on the back. "Do us good, buddy, to get out there in the fresh air and sunshine, mow the heck out that overgrowth along the roads. We gotta hack back that kudzu; it's probably gone crazy without us keeping it from crossin' the roads and covering everything up!"

Seth slowly placed his arms around Merle's broad shoulders. "You know it, Merle. We got lotsa work to do. See you in the morning."

Pearl shoved Seth out of the way, stood on tiptoes, and hugged and kissed Merle. "You wanna come in for supper, Merle?"

"Thank you, ma'am, Candy's waitin' on me. Another time maybe?"

"You got it, Merle. Thank you again for helping Seth. No way to repay you."

Merle drove off. It was as if a heavy boulder had slipped from his broad shoulders. With Seth out of jail, he felt better— but there was still more to do. *Job's not done. Need the answers. There's got to be justice for Seth and for those dead women.*

Candy moved around the kitchen preparing a low-fat, low-calorie dinner for Merle. He held Baby Maddy and clicked on the evening news. "Seth Wilkins was released from jail today into the arms of his mother, Pearl Wilkins, and his best friend, Merle Hucken," the news anchor intoned. "The D.A.'s office indicates Mr. Wilkins was not present at the time of the murder of Maybelle Jordan. Mr. Wilkins is not entirely exonerated, however. He faces felony charges regarding removal and illegal transport of a body. His court date will be in six weeks at which time he will learn the penalty and if he will serve a prison sentence."

Merle held the baby to his chest and said out loud, "Why'd our Seth-er do that stupid thing, Maddy? Move a body... dumbest thing, ever."

"In other news," the anchor continued, "Merle Hucken, who discovered the body of Maybelle Jordan, then exposed the illegal activities of former-sheriff Delbert Judd has been designated 'Citizen of the Year.' According to District Attorney Tanequa Milwood, he is being recognized for his assistance in apprehending Delbert Judd and for his numerous on-going civic contributions as volunteer firefighter, neighborhood-watch chairman, and committee chairman for cleanup of the Tahawsuh River."

Candy dropped a serving spoon, ran to Merle, and encircled him and the baby in her arms. "So proud of you, Merle, but please don't do anything that dangerous again. Promise?"

That night Merle lay awake, his mind racing. *Who killed those ladies? Someone who was seeing Maybelle Jordan, then maybe decided Edna Edgebert—who was always watching out her front window—might have seen him? One of the Maybelle's "boyfriends?"*

Had to be somebody she knew…

Restless, one salient question ran through Merle's thoughts: *Was it somebody who belongs to the Stags Lodge?*

CHAPTER 29

T HE NEXT DAY, SETH AND Merle resumed work. As soon as they arrived at the equipment garage, a welcoming crowd of co-workers greeted and cheered them. Adding to the joy of the day, the weather was crisp and beautifully clear—the beginnings of autumn—cool mornings and warm afternoons.

Along a broad stretch of highway just outside Fruitvale city limits, they unloaded mowers and other tools of their trade. Seth, looking relieved and relaxed, removed his cap and leaned against the truck. "It is so good to be out here, to be outside…"

Merle smiled at his old friend. "Yep, nothin' better…"

Seth settled into the seat of the wide-blade mower and started the engine. "Never thought this wonky-ol' mower would feel so good under my butt—but man, it's good to be doin' this again!"

At lunch, Seth and Merle pulled out lunch boxes. Seth bit into a biscuit stuffed with country ham and slaw. "Wow, mom's cookin'—this is great." He glanced over at Merle who was poking a fork into a container of salad. "Awful quiet, Merle. What's on your mind?"

Merle studied the horizon. "Who killed those ladies, Seth-er? Gotta know. Gotta know the bad guy's caught, that he's not out there, that he can't hurt any other person."

Seth popped open a Coke. He spoke slowly, thinking out loud. "One of the men Maybelle hustled? From what Ma's said, that'd be a bunch of guys. Ol' Maybelle was visited by most the men belongs to the Stags Lodge."

"Stags Lodge," Merle said. He shoved a forkful of salad greens into his mouth and gazed out at trees.

"Stags Lodge, what?"

"Dunno."

On Saturday, Merle hefted his bulk up steep steps at Stags Lodge POBS. He paused half way up to look at lettering under the sign: *Protective Order of Benevolent Stags*; beneath were the words *Fraternity and Charity*. He thought to himself, "This place's a local institution. Even my daddy belonged here once, couple of my uncles."

Merle entered the imposing red brick building and stood in the black-and-white tiled foyer. The clack-sound of a billiard ball could be heard from a room on the right. Merle found a group of men, cues in hand, enjoying a game. A gentleman looked up and catching sight of Merle said, "Well, look who's here! Citizen-of-the-Year, Merle Hucken!" The group surged forward to shake Merle's hand.

"Thanks, sirs, nice to be invited to visit your fine establishment."

"Yep, Merle," a gray-haired portly man said, "we hope you'll join us, be a Stag member. We'd like you to be a part of our organization!"

A familiar man stepped forward, "Yes, Merle, we Stags do good works—so this is right down your alley—'cuz you help your neighbors, volunteer. And by the way, Merle, can you sing? Looking for a fill-in for my barbershop quartet."

Merle suddenly recognized the skinny, big-eared fellow.

"Yes, sir, I remember you sang at the poor murdered woman's memorial service."

"Yes, we sang then." The man chuckled, his Adam's apple bobbing. "Unfortunately, Cal had a little problem that day… barfed up his breakfast. Wasn't a pretty sight."

The others snorted and guffawed. "Yep, Cal was mighty upset 'bout Maybelle's passing."

"But hey," a burly bystander added, "that's neither here nor there. What we need is to have Merle Hucken be a member of the Stags Lodge!" The group surrounded Merle with pats on his back and escorted him to the office to register.

Three weeks later, Merle was inducted as newest member of the Stags Lodge. The membership committee invited him out for a steak dinner. The skinny guy with the Adam's apple and big ears introduced him all around: "This here's Joe Stebbins, Dan Cleeson, and this is… and this here's Cal Medernicky—and meet Willy Lawson—and meet…"

"Nice to meet y'all," Merle said.

The evening was pleasant, the food and fellowship enjoyable. All the while, however, Merle felt a new sensitivity within himself—as if he now possessed some sort of detection system that scrutinized for unusual behavior, odd mannerisms, peculiar characteristics. Could one in this group of up-standing, church-going, civic-minded lodge members be the murderer of Maybelle Jordan and/or Edna Edgebert?

Most in the group were jovial, chatted easily, were gregarious. Merle enjoyed making conversation, discussing volunteer projects for the lodge.

Merle's newly-found "radar" detected two exceptions within the membership: Willy Lawson and Calvin Medernicky.

CHAPTER 30

RODNEY TAYLOR RETURNED MERLE'S CALL. "Hey, Merle, Mr. Citizen-of-the-Year! Good to hear from you. Glad you called, been meanin' to catch up with you."

"Yes, sir, just wondered if there'd been any leads on who killed Ms. Jordan and Ms. Edgebert. Any news?"

"Not a bit, Merle. Asked that same question of the D.A., Ms. Milwood. Nothing to report, I'm afraid. Bad guy—or guys—still out there. Unfortunately."

"Well, I was hopin' for some news—good news, that they'd found a murderer. Do you suppose it's someone right here in town, right under our noses, so to speak?"

"Likely, it is, Merle. We just need to find the guy with a motive… someone who was pushed over the edge enough to do such a terrible thing. Oh, and by the way, Merle, that young EMT who looked after you the night we arrested Delbert Judd—he's asked me twice how you're doing. Your sky-high blood pressure worried him. He seems to think you're a walking time-bomb, Merle. You taking care of yourself?"

"Uh, oh… not you guys, too! Candy and her mom Viv are after me to watch my weight. Hey, I know I'm fat and outta shape. Candy's got me watchin' carbs and all. I've lost some pounds, but guess that's like a cup o' water outta the ocean!" Merle laughed his hee-hah-hee.

"Hey, keep workin' on it, Merle. Need to stay healthy to

make sure you see that pretty baby girl of yours graduate from school."

"I know you're right, Rod. I'm on it! Tell that young EMT, Daryl, not to worry about me. And say, keep me posted on the murder investigation… will ya now?"

"You got it, Merle. Maybe we'll need you to wear a wire again!"

"Only if my blood pressure's lower!"

Rodney Taylor laughed and said goodbye.

Merle's phone rang again. Alvin Clegg. "Hey, Al, good to hear from you! What's up?

"Merle, I just thought I'd tell you about an encounter I had last Saturday in my art gallery. May not mean anything at all, but I'm just uneasy about a fellow named Cal Medernicky."

"Tell me more," Merle replied.

"First of all, he was something of a wreck—messy, looked like he hadn't showered for a week. And unmistakable that he'd been drinking, smelled of booze, blood-shot eyes. He was a mess. The worst part is he asked odd questions about my Aunt May… and made peculiar statements about your mother-in-law."

"What kind of questions?"

"Did I think Maybelle was in hell? Did I think she paid for her sins? He said maybe she needed to die, that she was not a good woman. That was bad enough, but then he went on to say, 'There were still good women in the world. There are good women like Ms. Vivian Smith.' Merle, when he mentioned your mother-in-law, I got worried!"

Merle's heart pounded. "I had a bad feelin' about that guy. Thanks for telling me, Al."

When Merle concluded the call, he thought, "What do I do with this information? How do I keep a crazy man away from my family?"

Merle dialed SBI Agent Rodney Taylor again. He then called

District Attorney Tanequa Milwood. He was surprised at how quickly they took his calls.

Merle directed his pickup into a gas station; and as he pumped regular into the rusty vehicle, he noticed a fellow Stag at a nearby pump. When the tank was full, he strolled over to greet the man. "Mornin', I'm Merle Hucken. Believe I met you at Stags Lodge a week or so ago."

"Hey, Merle," the soft-spoken man said. "Yes, we've met. I'm Willy Lawson."

"Good to see ya, Willy. Hey, nice car you got there! New?"

"Yes, sir, had a couple of weeks now."

"You been a Stags member long time, Willy?"

"Ummm, five—maybe six years. Me and my cousin joined together."

"What do you do for livin', Willy?"

"Work for the county. Criminal Records Division."

"Sounds like interesting work."

"It's okay. Lotsa bureaucratic detail. Sometimes interesting; sometimes not."

"Well, nice seeing you again." The two shook hands; and as Merle turned to leave, he asked, "You said you joined with your cousin. Who's that?"

Willy responded, "Cal Medernicky."

CHAPTER 31

MERLE WAS UNEASY, ALSO WEARY, having put in a long day at work. He opened the door to the doublewide and sank to a chair at the table. Viv arrived right behind him with an armload of groceries. "Hey, Merle, Candy and the baby are over at Marie Chung's. Told Candy I'll put together some dinner for us."

"You're putting another jewel in your crown, Granny Viv." He stood. "Let me get in the shower, but before I do—do you know a couple of guys—Calvin Medernicky and Willy Lawson?"

Viv pulled a carton of milk from the grocery bag and laughed out loud. "Ev-er-y-body knows Calvin and Willy! You remember the guy who sang with the quartet at Maybelle's service? The one we heard losing his lunch outside? That's Calvin Medernicky. And Willy is Cal's cousin."

"What's their story?"

Viv continued talking as she sorted and stowed the groceries. "Where to start…? Let me go waaaaay back, to school days. Willy and Calvin are cousins, as I said, and when we were all in school, those two were the odd-men out. I mean, they just did not click with anyone except with each other."

"Why was that?"

"I honestly do not know. It's just that they were kinda strange, did not make any friends, so they only hung out with each other. In high school, neither of them could get a date. As a matter of fact, I was invited out by Calvin once… had a miserable time.

Went just because I felt bad for him. Tried hard to like him, but he's really different. He was never a good student; I kinda think he's just not that smart. Don't think he ever learned a trade or was interested in higher education…"

"I talked to the cousin, Willy Lawson. He doesn't seem so bad."

"Well, Willy managed to find a girlfriend and got married. His wife's a piece o'work, I'm told. And, far as I know, Willy's got a good job with the county. The interesting part is that after Willy married, Calvin was really on his own. He's from a comfortable family, never had to work all that hard, so he just hung around town, stayed kind of a loner. Someone told me recently his two best friends are beer and vodka."

"That's too bad."

"Yes, he's a very sad story."

"Do you think he's dangerous—mentally, I mean?"

"Nah, Cal's just off by a few inches. Harmless."

Later, that evening, Merle and Viv pulled into the parking lot behind the Stags Lodge. "I sure appreciate you going with me to this event, Viv."

"Ladies Night at Stags Lodge—whooo hoo—what could be more fun than that!"

"I know you're jokin', Viv, but you know some of these old guys—ummm, sorry, I mean 'older' gentlemen. Candy would be bored to tears doing this. She's happier at home with Maddy."

"Merle, you know I'm happy to tag along with you—might be interestin' to run across some old classmates, their wives or ex-wives, nieces, nephews, cousins. Who knows who'll be here? In a small place like Fruitvale, there's always someone who knows you or you know them! It'll be fun."

Merle removed the keys from the ignition and paused. "Viv, I know this sounds kinda nutty, but I think the murderer of the two ladies could be a member here. Something tells me he could be standin' right in front of us."

Viv looked serious, swallowed nervously. "That's a terrifying thought, Merle."

"You still okay to do this?"

Viv looked directly into Merle's sky-blue eyes. "You betcha, son."

Viv took Merle's arm as they entered the Stags Lodge ballroom. Viv, wearing a smart sweater and slacks, her silver-streaked hair done nicely, glanced around and immediately recognized a number of people. "Oh look, there's Angela Cleeson—haven't seen her in ages. This'll be old home week, Merle."

Viv let loose of Merle's arm and began working the room. She greeted people and was immediately surrounded with chatting, laughing people. She asked about family, neighbors, church acquaintances. It was clear to Merle Viv knew many from her school years—or was acquainted with an ex-wife, a cousin, a co-worker. He watched her greet Willy Lawson who introduced her to his wife—a large woman with dyed burgundy red hair and wearing a Hawaiian print dress. "Guess your son-in-law's some kind of hero!" Mrs. Lawson said.

"Well now, he's a hero in our house," Viv responded, laughing.

Merle stayed near but struck up a conversation with the Adam's apple guy. "Hey, Merle, you ready to join my barbershop quartet?" he asked. "Need a good tenor; bet you can hit some of those notes!"

Merle laughed. "I'm afraid not, sir, not a singer, but seemed like you had a real good group that day you sang at Ms. Jordan's service. Even with Cal Medernicky not feeling so good."

"He was definitely under the weather, but more than that, he was really bummed out about Maybelle. He was quite fond of the ol' gal." The man's Adam's apple bobbed up and down in the loose collar of his shirt. "Now he never shows for our practices. Think he's still grieving for Maybelle."

"How's that?"

The man tipped his thumb to his lips as if to say, "Hittin' the bottle these days."

"That's too bad. An' you're sayin' he was real close to Maybelle Jordan?"

"He thought he was."

Merle glanced around the ballroom. He spied Viv talking with—none other than—Calvin Medernicky. Merle headed in their direction; and as he approached, he heard Viv saying, "Thank you, Calvin. That's so kind of you, but you know what, I'm widowed, yes, but I still feel married to Candy's dad, so I'm just not interested in going out. I do appreciate the invitation, Cal, I really do. I hope you understand."

Viv sensed Merle as her side. "Hey, Merle, we best get on home. Candy'll need help with the baby." She turned to Calvin Medernicky. "Lovely to see you, Cal. You take care now."

Merle took Viv's arm and sensed she was trembling. He could see veins in her neck pulsating. "You okay, Viv?"

When they were settled in Viv's car, she seemed calmer. "Calvin is still a really odd duck. The first thing he said to me was, "I understand you're a 'widdah woman.' Widdah woman?! Who says that? It was as if he thought because I was widowed and without a man that I would be interested in going out with him! Not on your life!"

"Did you feel pressured by him—or threatened?"

"No. Just very uncomfortable."

The next day, Sunday, Viv and Candy returned from church. "How'd Maddy do while we were gone?" Candy asked Merle.

"Oh, we had a grand ol' time. We looked at a picture book; 'course Maddy wanted to put the book in her mouth and taste it."

"Merle," Viv interrupted, "when I got in the car this morning,

I coulda sworn Calvin Medernicky was in a car parked down the street from my house."

"Then," Candy added, "he was waiting outside church when we came out. I kinda feel he followed us home."

Merle handed the baby to Candy and strode to the door and down the porch steps. He looked up and down the street but saw no Calvin Medernicky. Back indoors, he felt a worried, sick feeling creeping into his gut. *Are my girls in danger?*

CHAPTER 32

"BYE, MAMA," CANDY SAID AS she pulled on her jacket. "Bye, pretty Maddy. Mommy be back from the doctor's in no time." She grabbed her handbag and left for her appointment.

"Let's have bath time, baby girl," Viv was saying when she heard something out front of the mobile home. "Trash pickup's awful early," she thought. Suddenly the door flew wide open, and Calvin Medernicky stood in the doorway. He swung the door closed and pulled a small handgun from his coat pocket. He cradled it like a gift in the palms of his hands.

"Well now, Miss Vivian, how ya doin' today?"

Viv held the baby tight to her body. She could not speak; she felt faint. At last, she managed to say, "Calvin, what is it you want?"

"You know, now don't ya, Miss Vivian? Now that you're a single lady, I can be your true love."

"Calvin, I've told you I have no interest. Ronald was my true love and always will be." She looked at the gun, her heart tripping staccato. "Why do you have a gun? Are you going to kill me? What have I ever done to you?"

"Oh, no, Miss Viv, I have no reason to kill you. That's not why I'm here. It's just that I need you to come along with me, and I expected maybe you'd be some reluctant. This here gun's just to encourage you some. So, you come along now and get yourself and that baby a warm sweater, 'cuz, we're goin' in the car now."

"No, you can't take us anywhere—especially this innocent baby girl! She's not to be taken away from her home!"

"Now, Miss Vivian, I'm saying you and the baby will come along with me now. Just like a real family. The baby and her granny and her granddad. That's us." Viv stood frozen. After a minute, Cal spat words through yellow teeth. "Woman, I'm in charge now. I'm the man of the house, and you do as you're told."

Suddenly Viv's fear ebbed, and she was enveloped by an unusual calm. She pulled a sweater over Maddy's chubby arms. Her jacket lay over the back of a chair, and she grabbed it along with Maddy's baby blanket. "Okay," she said, "but if you harm this baby, we are not a family. Do you understand me, Calvin? You will treat this baby with respect. If we're to be a family, you are not to hurt Maddy."

Calvin looked thoughtful and nodded. "Yes, Miss Vivian, I'll take good care of this grandbaby girl of —ours." He chuckled as he herded Viv, with the baby clinging to her, to the door. Viv turned suddenly. "We can't go in your car. Your car doesn't have a car seat. A baby has to be in a proper car seat."

"You got one in your car, Miss Vivian?"

"Yes."

"Where's your car keys?"

"My purse. On that chair."

He found the keys, took Viv by the arm. She remained remarkably steady as they rounded the side of the home. He opened the rear door of Viv's car. Viv placed the baby in her car seat and tucked the blanket around her. She started to climb in beside her.

"No! You sit up front with me like we're her grandparents takin' the babe for a ride." Calvin said, his voice a nasal snarl.

Viv obediently closed the rear door and settled in the front seat. Calvin removed two lengths of dirty rope from his coat pocket. "Put your hands together, and put your feet together." He tucked the gun under his armpit and wound the rope tightly around Viv's hands, then her ankles.

Viv glanced around at the house of the next-door neighbors. She prayed someone would see her being abducted, but the Greens worked long hours—would not be home until dark. She began to cry.

"Aw, now, for cryin' out loud, woman, we just goin' for a ride out to our country house. No need to get your knickers all in a knot." He piled into the driver's side of the car. "Just relax now—enjoy our little family bein' together." He snapped the seat belt around Viv and started the engine.

Viv was hit with a nauseating smell of alcohol, his bad breath, his unwashed clothing. Through tears, she asked, "Why are you doing this, Cal? What good is this?"

"Why, Miss Vivian, I'm shocked you don't understand. We just need some qual-i-ty time together. We were always meant to be together." He headed to the highway and turned south. "A good woman like you, Miss Vivian, knows how to be true, to be faithful."

"I've told you—more than once—I still feel married to Ronald and will never remarry again."

"And I'm tellin' you, and I'm tellin' you, this is exactly why we need to spend some time at our country place, so's you understand it's me you need to be true to…"

Viv did not speak. Her mind raced—how to get away from this mentally unstable man, to keep Baby Maddy safe, to survive. Suddenly, she heard herself speaking directly to Calvin: "What you're doing here, Calvin, is a serious crime. Kidnapping. Kidnapping two people. When they catch you, you will go to prison, maybe the gas chamber. Calvin, they execute people for kidnapping."

Calvin Medernicky burst into laughter. Tears rolled down his puffy cheeks, dripped from his bulbous nose. Viv turned her head away from the stench of his foul breath. He wiped his rough hand across his face to clear the tears. He kept chuckling. Suddenly, without a hint of a mood change, he spat angry words through his teeth. "An' you think I care 'bout that? Already did away with two worthless women."

Viv, her blood running cold, an electric-shock shiver running through her body, said nothing.

Calvin glanced over at her as if he expected her to register surprise. When he saw Viv's non-reaction, he continued, "Could not stand Edna. She was snotty to me one-too-many times, tellin' ya. Even way back when we was all in school. Nosy bitch too, she was." He changed lanes as if this was an every-day sort of conversation. "An' Maybelle was nothin' but a whore, not true to nobody." He glanced in the rearview mirror as if what he was saying was nothing more than the day's news. "Should give me a medal for doing 'way with them. Waste o' time, those two no-good women."

Again, Viv did not react. She stared ahead at the cars in front of them. After a few minutes, she again heard her own matter-of-fact voice, "You must have had more reasons than Maybelle's reputation to kill her."

Calvin spoke as if they were discussing the weather. "She told me—that night—to not come 'round her house no more, that she was 'weary' of me. Weary of me! Now, Miss Vivian, I had brought her lots and lots of that red wine she liked. Musta brought her cases of it. I couldn't stand it, but she liked it. When she tol' me to just stay away, that she was tired of me, didn't want my company no more, I grabbed one of those big liter bottles and bashed her with it. Taught her a lesson, I did."

Viv, again in her self-induced state of calm, asked, "What did you do with that bottle, Calvin—the one you hit her with?"

"I dunno—tossed it in some dumpster behind the convenience store, I guess."

Cal turned off the highway and into a narrow, rutted road through pine forest. Viv sensed they were southeast of Fruitvale somewhere along the lake. She could see the sun gleaming on fragments of the lake as they passed through trees. The mid-morning air was cool and crisp, a clear November morning.

Calvin's confession terrified Vi. She agonized. *I'm with a killer… my poor baby Maddy… we're with a killer.*

CHAPTER 33

MERLE AND SETH'S WORKDAY WAS underway, and they'd completed two miles of mowing. The morning sun warmed the cool air; it was the kind of day they always enjoyed when they had many miles of mowing ahead of them.

"Great weather," Seth observed. "S'posed to rain later tonight, but we'll be done by the time it hits."

Merle did not answer.

"Merle? Looks like your head is somewhere else."

"Worried. I think there's a crazy guy named Calvin Medernicky stalking Candy's mom. Last couple of days, he's been calling at her house— 'unknown caller' on the phone ID, then he just hangs on the line. He's followed her to church and to the Piggly Wiggly. The DA and Rodney Taylor—you 'member the SBI agent—know about him."

Merle reached down to answer his cell phone. "Just a sec', it's Candy. Hi, sweetie… what? What? Call Rodney Taylor! Call Tanequa Milwood!" Merle's ruddy cheeks turned ashen. He yelled into the phone, "I'm comin' home right now!"

"Good grief, Merle—what the heck's goin' on?" Seth wore a worried look.

"Candy can't find Viv and Baby Maddy. They're not at our house or at Viv's place. Something tells me Viv's in trouble!"

The two friends worked furiously to stow the equipment

back on to the flatbed truck. They raced to the equipment garage, breaking all speed limits.

"I'll tell the boss what's goin' on an' then I'll come to your house a quick as can. I'll stay with Candy while you find out what's happening."

"Good," Merle breathed out. He was perspiring, his heart pounding. He ran to his truck. The old vehicle backfired twice, adding to his anxiety.

At home, Merle hustled up the steps to find Candy pale and shaking, frightened. "When I came back from the doctor, Mama's not here, nor the baby. Car's gone, but her purse is still on the chair. If she had to go somewhere, she'd have left a note or called!"

Within minutes, the street outside the Hucken home was filled with vehicles. Rodney Taylor ran up the steps followed by Seth. "Tanequa Milwood's on the phone with the FBI—they're sending a team, be here ASAP."

"FBI?" Merle said, his voice cracking.

"This is a kidnapping, Merle," Agent Taylor said calmly, "a federal offense."

Alvin Clegg drew up in his shiny BMW and joined the group. "I heard Miss Vivian is missing. I'm worried it might be the crazy guy who was in my gallery."

Seth was amazed. "Boy, news travels fast in Fruitvale."

"Calvin Medernicky," Merle said. "We find him, we'll find Viv and the baby." He was silent for a moment. "We need to talk to his cousin Willy Lawson."

Rodney Taylor dialed his cell. "Send two agents to find Willy Lawson. He works at the county courthouse. Bring him to the Hucken residence ASAP. Tell him we need his help to find his cousin, Calvin Medernicky."

Candy began to cry. "I'm so scared! Mama and Maddy are in danger! That crazy man will hurt them!"

Seth spoke to calm her. "They'll find them, Candy. There's a bunch of great people here to help."

Merle, flushed and sweaty, his head swimming, said. "Sether's right, sweetie. Good people care."

In short order, two SBI agents arrived with a trembling, ashen Willy Lawson. "I haven't seen Cal today," he said quickly. Another agent added, "Checked the Medernicky residence. No one there, and no car in the garage."

"That's because that car there," Willy said, pointing to a late model Buick parked on the street, "is Cal's car." He sank to the porch step as if faint and held his head in his hands.

"Mr. Lawson," Rodney Taylor said, "We have reason to believe Calvin Medernicky has taken Ms. Vivian Smith and the Hucken baby against their will—that he may not be thinking rationally. Where would he be likely to go?"

"Where did Cal take Viv and the baby?" Merle demanded. When Willy did not respond, Merle asked again, "Where, man? Think!" He did not realize he was shouting.

Willy looked up, a startled, glazed look in his eyes. "Maybe the cabin."

"What cabin?" Rodney Taylor demanded.

"Family has a wreck of an old cabin back of the lake, 'bout 25 miles south. We used it for deer hunting. Nobody's used it for years… not sure if it's even still standing." Willy looked ill, grimaced, clutched his chest as if having a heart attack.

"You're gonna tell us exactly how to get there—and now!" Merle yelled. His patience was at breaking point.

CHAPTER 34

CALVIN MEDERNICKY MADE A RIGHT turn from the road they'd traveled along the lake. Viv's car rocked as they drove over deep ruts and foot-high pine seedlings attempting to establish themselves on the narrow lane. Viv, now knowing she was held custody by a murderer, surrounded herself with all the calm she could.

Cal chuckled. "You know, Miss Viv, you and I got some fixin' to do on this old place. We'll get us some paint and pretty it up some, make a right nice country house for us to get away to from time to time. You could plant you some real pretty flowers out front." He drew the car up to a rough-hewn shack. The dilapidated building sagged to the right, the porch at a slant. "Just needs some good hammering here and there, an' it'll be a right nice place again. Let me show you around, Miss Viv. I know you're gonna really like our little place—for us to be together."

Baby Maddy had begun to fuss. "Waaaa, waaah!" she wailed and flapped her chubby hands on the car seat.

"The baby needs her diaper changed, Calvin. She's going to need to be fed! She still nurses twice a day; she's not weaned yet. She needs her mother, Calvin!" Viv spoke as forcefully as she could. "You're already doing harm to this baby by keeping her in a wet diaper and away from her mother!" Viv gave Calvin a furious look.

"Now, now, pretty lady. Aren't we pretty when we're mad

at poor ol' Calvin? Here I take you out to our nice little country place, and that's how you talk. My, my… we're havin' our first spat."

"I'm telling you the baby needs to be nursed by her mother."

"And, woman, I'm telling you she'll be fine. I'm her grampy, an' I'll teach her to drink outta a real cup."

Viv said nothing more.

"Now, Miss Viv, tell you what we're gonna do," Calvin continued. "I'm gonna untie your pretty ankles so's you can walk in our nice place here, an' I'm gonna just unlatch the baby in her seat here and bring her inside with us…" He untied the rope from Viv's feet. "An' I know you're not gonna be takin' off nowheres because we're 'bout 30 miles from anywhere there's any other folks, an' you don't wanna get lost in these big ol' dark woods, now do ya?"

Viv took a deep breath and stood from the car. She followed Calvin to the porch, then took one step at a time on to the porch. Calvin turned and waited for her; his arms holding the very fussy baby in her car seat. He pushed open the unlocked door and set the baby down on a faded easy chair. A mini-mushroom cloud of dust rose from the chair. Maddy sneezed, then coughed. She burst into a loud wail.

"She needs to be diapered and fed, Calvin! This is abuse to leave a baby like this!" Viv snapped.

Calvin actually looked hurt. "I'm not gonna hurt our grandbaby, Viv. You know better than that. Here, you sit here, and let me just tie your feet together again—just to be sure you won't be goin' nowheres."

Viv sank to a rickety ladderback chair that groaned as it took her weight. Calvin quickly tied her ankles. Viv looked around the living space of the cabin. The creaking floor slanted; a crack in the roof let in a streak of mid-day sun. The gap in the roof was an avenue for rain that—over time—had dampened everything and left streaks of mold and mildew. Maddy began to shriek.

"Untie my hands, Calvin! At least let me hold her so she won't cry so hard!" Viv yelled.

CHAPTER 35

WILLY LAWSON CAME TO HIS senses and provided detailed directions to the hunting cabin, and Rodney Taylor—with the help of four FBI agents—organized a team of law enforcement. Three large black vans arrived. Merle's heart thudded as he caught a glimpse of assault weapons and all sort of police gear. Within an hour, the stone-faced team was ready. "You come along, Merle. You can maybe negotiate Viv's release," Rodney said.

"As if you could keep me away," Merle said, his heart racing. He turned to Seth and Alvin. "You guys look after Candy?"

"You got it, Merle," Seth replied.

One of the agents turned to Merle, "On the way out, I'll give you a short-course in negotiating with an unhinged person. You need to know some techniques in case you end up talking with the guy. If he wants to talk to you, you gotta talk his talk, Merle—let on you understand his reasons for doing what he's doing—even though you know what he's doing is wrong and dangerous. Still have to show him some respect."

Merle said quickly, "Just tell me what I need to do."

Rodney Taylor continued, "On arriving, first thing we do is stay well back and assess—in case there's gunfire."

"Gunfire?"

"A hunting cabin has weapons, Merle. Guy might have a gun

on him. But not to worry, Chet Edwards will be on scene. He helped last time—remember when he took out Sheriff Judd."

"Took out the sheriff?"

"Yeah, guy's a crack shot."

"Crack shot?"

"Sharpshooter."

"Sharpshooter?"

"Sniper, Merle. Chet Edwards's the guy who knocked down the sheriff that night in the woods."

Merle's heart pounded, his pulse raced. *A sniper, guns, and my baby girl and Granny Viv. This is the worst—how did it ever come to this?*

The late afternoon November day drew to a close with hazy sun slipping past the pine forest. The lake gleamed red and gold for an instant as the sun fell below the horizon. Light in the derelict cabin ebbed; a fine mist drifted through gaps in the roof.

The baby had cried herself to sleep, her chubby body draped over the side of the car seat. She twitched and whimpered. In his delusional state, Calvin tucked the blanket around her. He stood back, tipped his greasy gray head and smiled—as if he were a devoted grandparent tending to his grandchild.

Viv, her heart breaking not to be able to comfort and care for the baby, tried to move, shifted her aching back to restore circulation. She surveyed the space and once again, for the hundredth time, considered how to get loose of the restraints on her hands and legs. A rusty cast-iron skillet rested on top of the ancient wood-burning stove. *If only I could get that heavy pan, I'd whack the livin' daylights out of the idiot.*

Cal moved around the cabin, muttering as he looked for a light source. "Used to have a good ol' kerosene lantern somewhere…" He knocked over something, waking the baby. She began to fuss again, rubbing her eyes with back of her chubby hands. Her fussing became a cry; the cry became a wail.

"Calvin!" Viv cried out. "You must let me hold that baby! She's cold and wet and hungry!"

"Wait! I hear something outside," Calvin said, his hand suspended in air.

A high-pitched male voice shouted, "Mr. Medernicky! Mr. Medernicky! It's Merle Hucken! I brought the baby some diapers, some baby food. I know you just overlooked bringing that along. Lemme just leave these things on the porch so's you can take good care of Baby Maddy."

Merle waited; he heard Maddy crying which reassured him she was in there, but almost propelled him up the steps to snatch her and Viv away to safety. It was all he could do to hold himself back. He called out loudly again, "Mr. Medernicky!"

Viv's heart pounded, and she said a silent prayer. *Oh, please be careful of this man, Merle—he has a gun!* She collected herself and told Calvin, "If you get the diapers, Calvin, I'll change the baby real quick and get her fed, then she'll be fine and won't fuss so much."

Anger grabbed at Calvin, and he yelled, "Shut up, woman!"

Viv wondered if he was thrown by the fact that Merle, all newly-trim 270 pounds and six feet, six inches of him was standing outside Calvin's sanctuary.

"Mr. Medernicky!" Merle called again. "I'm not going to bother you and come on in. I'll just wait while you get ready to get these things for the baby. Lemme know if you wanna come out, sir."

Calvin hustled his portly body to the crooked door that separated him from the outside world and yelled, "You just go on home now, Merle. We're fine in here. Don't need no help. You just go on home now. I'll take care of the baby and Miss Vivian."

Calvin yelled at the top of his lungs to be heard over the cries of Baby Maddy, "You go on home right now!"

"Okay, Mr. Medernicky. Sounds like Maddy needs her diaper changed. She's probably needin' some supper now. Sure sounds like it! Tell you what—I'll leave these things here on the porch—so's they're right handy." Merle waited for a response. When none came, he said as loudly as he could, "Anything you need for me to do for you? You want I should help you anyway?" No response. "Mr. Medernicky? Sir?"

Merle's voice comforted Viv. She settled back into her cocoon of calm. "Isn't that good of Merle to bring the baby things?" she said, quietly. "He's such a good daddy to Maddy—does everything for his sweet baby girl." She waited then said, softly, "A grampy meets the need of his granddaughter, doesn't he, Cal?"

Calvin had begun pacing. Agitated, restless, then stopping abruptly, then shifting from one foot to the other, then pacing again, he turned to Viv and spat words. "You just stay outta this, woman! This is man's talk. No woman talk allowed. You hear me?"

"Yes, sir," Viv breathed out. Maddy's wails were subdued for a moment. She coughed and sputtered and kicked her baby legs.

Merle's voice again, "Mr. Medernicky, please take care of Viv and Maddy. They're so important to my wife Candy and me. We love and care about them, so if you're gonna keep them here with you, please take good care of them. And the baby needs these diapers and food. Please come out and get them off the porch. I'm leaving them right here for you." By this time, he was at the porch steps.

"Placing the things on the porch now, sir. Is there anything else I can do for you, Mr. Medernicky?"

No response from inside the cabin. "Okay, sir, I'll be leavin' now."

Merle descended four steps down from the porch. He turned around and called out again, "Sir! Was just thinkin'… since I'm here, maybe—and only if this works for you—you could hand me the baby, and I'll quick-like change her diaper and calm her down some. Maybe feed her a little bit. Then she'd be ready to nap. Might be easier for you!" Maddy kept up her litany of wails, sputtering, choking, now screaming.

Calvin suddenly shuffled to the baby and hoisted her up in the car seat. He flung open the door, kicked it aside, and staggered onto the porch. "Take this damn brat of yours, and leave me and Miss Vivian alone—we're just fine without you and this bawlin' kid."

In a bound, Merle was at the door. Maddy saw him and raised her little arms as if to say, "Hold me, Daddy!"

"Ah, baby girl," Merle breathed out as he slid his arms under the car seat. He looked directly at Calvin Medernicky and said, calmly, "Thank you, sir. I'll take care of her so's you can get some rest. Takin' care of a cryin' baby can be a real chore." He turned and strode down the steps, made a sharp left turn. His long strides propelled him away from the shack in seconds.

As Calvin Medernicky turned his back and grabbed the creaking door, a crack of gunfire from the rifle of Chet Edwards rang out. Calvin Medernicky fell clutching his left hip. His shrieks pierced the cool evening air.

CHAPTER 36

A T HOME, MERLE HAD FORGOTTEN he was still wearing a bulletproof vest. He pulled off his damp sweatshirt, unbuckled the itchy contraption, and sighed relief as he handed it to one of the agents. "I never wanna wear this thing again," he said shaking his head.

Rodney Taylor and Tanequa Milwood had just finished taking Viv's statement about the day's event. She related in detail Calvin Medernicky's confession of killing Maybelle Jordan and Edna Edgebert. Exhausted, she sipped tea. Candy hovered, "Can I get you anything, Mama?" Baby Maddy, back in her crib, slept soundly.

"No, darlin'," Viv responded. "Just glad to be here with you and know all this fuss is over and done with!"

"Merle," Tanequa interjected, "we've had another confession. Willy Lawson. He came clean that he had altered the time of death on Ms. Jordan's death certificate. Seems his cousin Calvin Medernicky had paid him $25,000 to do so. We know now that Medernicky was at the crime scene and is the murderer. He wanted the time of death to be later, so he would not be a suspect. Willy Lawson fixed it to look like Ms. Jordan was killed early morning rather than when Medernicky was at her house. When we learned Seth Wilkins was not there at the time of death noted on the document—the actual time being about 1:30 a.m.—

it threw me off for a bit, but it all makes sense now and ties up another loose end."

"Lawson had both opportunity and motivation," added Rodney Taylor. "He had access to the records, and accommodating his cousin meant he now had enough money for a new car."

"And one more piece of good news, Merle," Tanequa continued, "I've petitioned the court to dismiss charges against Seth Wilkins—that all things considered, it does not serve justice to bring him to trial. He'll be on probation for one year, do community service. The judge took into account his clean record and his volunteer firefighting."

Merle, exhausted, managed a weak smile and could only say, "Ah, Seth-er's gonna be okay. That's so good."

He stood, drew up to his full height and extended his right hand to Agent Taylor and his left to Tanequa Milwood. "I wanna thank the both of you. You caught the bad guys, an' now my family's safe. An' my best friend's not in jail accused of something he did not do."

Rodney Taylor said quickly, "Couldn't have done it without Merle Hucken."

"Agreed," the D.A. added, "Merle Hucken deserves the credit."

CHAPTER 37

ERLE AND SETH RETURNED TO work. Each felt renewed, relieved, happy to back outdoors with the mowers rumbling beneath them. "Wow, look at that kudzu," Merle said, "what's with that stuff that it grows so crazy fast?"

"Has us to keep it under control," Seth said as he sat in the seat of the wide-blade mower. He started the engine. "What a great day," he hollered as he drove away from Merle and the equipment truck. "Watch out for yellow jackets, ol' buddy!"

"You betcha, Seth-er!" Merle flapped his cap and smiled. "You betcha!"

A few weeks later, Merle arrived at home after a long day of work. Looking relaxed and happy, Candy greeted him with a hug and a kiss. She wore an emerald green blouse and neat jeans; her shiny hair was piled atop her head. She held Maddy. "Say hi to your hard-working hero-daddy, baby girl!" Maddy raised up her arms for Merle to hold her.

"Come to your sweaty daddy, sweetie," he said as he took her in his arms. "Your mommy sure does look pretty this evenin', Miss Maddy! She throwin' us over for some other guy?"

Candy laughed and turned to finish preparing the evening

meal. Merle placed Maddy in her high chair and headed to the shower.

Later, Candy pulled a pan of roast chicken and vegetables from the oven. She transferred them to a platter, tossed a green salad, and set the table. Merle watched as she readied the meal.

"You are lookin' so fine, my beautiful wife!" Merle said as he took a chair at the table.

"I'm feeling good, Merle. Feeling so much better."

"What's changed to make you feel better?"

Candy sat, pulled a napkin from the table, and smoothed it in her lap. "Maybe it's all about counting blessings—having a wonderful family—you, Mama, Maddy. Having good friends like Marie Chung, having good neighbors. But, too, it's understanding that depression is a real illness, but it can be treated and managed. Finally, I had the courage to face it head-on—my doctor helped; Marie helped me find a support group. Bottom line is—I understand myself better. I can manage better now."

Merle listened. "I count my blessing every day, sweetie, that I have you." He stared at her with tearful eyes. Candy filled Merle's plate. He looked down at his plate. "Great dinner, sweetie," he said as he tucked into the roast chicken.

"Need to tell you one more thing, Merle. Talked with a friend of Marie's, Katie Bonnedice, and she offered me a job at her chocolate shop. It's new… in downtown Fruitvale. The store's called 'Everything Chocolate.'"

Merle put his fork down and took the napkin to his mouth. His eyes were wide, questioning. "A chocolate store? Sounds like a dangerous place to me."

"It's a really nice operation. There's a kitchen in the back, and they make everything by hand—nut clusters, fudge, truffles. Most fun is they mold chocolate—not only things like Easter bunnies, but guitars, little pianos, even garden tools made out of chocolate. Very creative, and the shop smells divine when you walk in—this warm chocolate smell just floats over you.”

“She’s offered you a job in this dangerous place? What would you do?”

“Little bit of everything. Help in the kitchen making the chocolates, she’ll teach me… and work the front of the store, selling, fixing displays… Merle, what do you think?”

“I gotta question. How does that fit with this healthy eating you got me started on—cuttin’ out sugar, watchin’ the carbs? How’m I supposed to keep off these eighty-five pounds I just took off? I mean, with you comin’ home smellin’ like chocolate?”

“You remember Mama’s lecture about ‘all good things in moderation?’ Doesn’t mean we can’t eat sweets once in a while—we just have to take care not to overdo.”

When Merle did not respond, Candy asked, “What do you think, Merle? The pay’s pretty good, Maddy’s Granny Viv’s ready to fill in around here… Merle?”

Merle took Candy’s hand in his and looked deep into her green eyes. “I think I got me a talented, beautiful wife who’s capable of doing lots of interestin’ things. Go for it, my beauty!”

CHAPTER 38

"**S**ETH-ER! WAKE UP! FIRE AT 800 Jefferson. Judge's place. I'm headin' out now!" Merle yelled into his cell phone. "Wake up, Seth-er. Get to the station now!"

"Time is it, Merle?" Seth croaked, shaking off deep sleep.

"Early in the a.m., good buddy. Ummm… two-oh-five… to be exact. Get goin'… Station now!"

"Okay, okay!'"

Merle, bundled against the icy winter night, clicked off the phone and turned the ignition key in his pickup. The vehicle sputtered and groaned. "Come on, now," Merle breathed out. "Dad-gum-it! Know it's cold, and I don't wanna be out in this weather, but we gotta go save the judge's house!" He removed his foot from the gas pedal and waited. "Okay, ol' guy, I'll just wait you out. Take your time now… we don't have to hurry… we can just sit here and let the good judge's house burn down?" Merle waited. "Shall we try one more time, pickup, or you gonna just be ill with me? Okay, gonna give you another chance…"

Merle turned the key. The ignition ground a grating whirr, and the motor sat silent. "Look, old pickup o' mine, we've been through thick and thin together. I courted my beautiful wife Candy in you, I asked her to marry me in you, I brought home my sweet baby girl Maddy in you, you get me to work every day so I can feed my family…"

As if the old pickup heard Merle and awakened to the urgency of the situation, the motor turned over on the next try. In minutes, he arrived at the fire station and grabbed his gear. Seth and three other firefighters were a few minutes behind, grabbed their gear in rapid succession, and the Fruitvale volunteer fire team was on the way.

"One engine's already there, and the Mossville team's right behind," Jeremy yelled out as he hit the siren. "Gonna need all the help we can get. This is a bad one!"

Judge Milton Stebbins's stately brick home, a landmark dating back to the early twentieth-century, was under siege. The grandest of Fruitvale's residences, the house was a fiery pyre against the cold and clear winter sky. Orange-red feathers of flame licked out from windows; the heavy shake roof was engulfed.

The judge and his wife, shivering in their nightclothes, huddled under a blanket. Mrs. Stebbins wept; the judge looked old and fragile. They'd escaped their family home of forty years with scarce moments to spare——having experienced the nightmare of nightmares: to be awakened by a crackling sound, the acrid smell of smoke. A policewoman escorted them to a cruiser—sheltering them from the chill of the night.

Merle, Seth, and the crew of trained volunteer firefighters swung into action. Merle, now among the most fit and strong, used every ounce of his ability to knock back shrubbery and pull heavy hoses within feet of the flames. The firefighter assault continued for hours. By the light of morning, the house—the remains charred and steaming—was declared a total loss in spite of the firefighters' best efforts and expertise.

Later, at the fire station, the exhausted crew huddled over coffee. "That fire was set. We got arson here," Jeremy, the captain said. He rubbed his smoke-smudged face with his hands and suppressed a yawn. "Police are callin' in the SBI."

"Lookin' at the color of those flames, how they shot up so high, there had to be some kinda accelerant maybe spread around the perimeter of the house," said another weary firefighter.

The crew remained silent, sipped coffee, reflected on the night's hard work. At last, breaking the thoughtful silence, Seth asked, "Who'd burn down the judge's home?"

"Any number of guys the judge sent up to Central Prison or Butner… ol' Judge Stebbins's tough on criminals over the years. Put away some real bad ones," Jeremy replied.

Merle stretched out his arm and rubbed out muscle soreness in his shoulder. "Like those Korean guys who ran drugs." He shook his head. Profound sorrow crossed his usually sunny face. "And killed good man Jimmy Chung."

Quiet weariness returned. Again, it was Seth who spoke, "So, if they're all in jail, how'd they set a fire?"

If the team of firefighters had not been so exhausted, one would have teased Seth about another of his naive questions. The group gazed at Seth as if the answer were obvious. Finally, Merle offered, "Korean mafia—the Kkangpae?" He swirled the last of the coffee in his cup. "Judge Stebbins sent the Kim brothers straight to death row, handed out the toughest sentence there is. Maybe somebody wants revenge."

"Korean mafia. Thought we were done with those guys," Seth said as he glanced over at Merle.

Merle detected sadness and worry in his old friend's eyes; the mention of the Koreans brought back painful memories.

CHAPTER 39

THE NEXT DAY, SETH AND Merle prepared to work along Highway 50, an older stretch of road near Liston. They unloaded equipment from the state truck, their breath fogging forward on the wintry day.

"No traffic to speak of out here today," Merle said. "You wanna trim those branches hangin' over the pavement?"

"Sure… just a sec. Phone's ringing. Who could that be?" Seth retrieved his phone from his jacket pocket and pulled off a glove with his teeth. The cold morning had put a pink blush on his angular face, but when he saw the caller I.D., he blanched. With wide, questioning eyes, he looked up at Merle. "Who do we know at 'Real Good BBQ?'"

"Barbecue?" Merle's rosy face held a quizzical expression.

Seth answered, "Seth Wilkins here." He placed his gloved left hand on his head and spun in a circle.

"Soon Ha?"

CHAPTER 40

C ANDY HUCKEN, NEWEST EMPLOYEE OF Everything Chocolate, slid a tray of raspberry truffles into the display case. The chain of small bells attached to the shop door chimed. She looked up and recognized three ladies from Fruitvale Redeemer Baptist church.

"Mornin', ladies," she called out.

"Well, if'n it isn't Candy in the candy store!" A round, pleasant-looking woman called out.

Candy answered, "Yes, ma'am!"

All three stood for a moment to inhale. "My, that's a lovely smell," one lady exuded. "Just makes you wanna a big piece of chocolate, just smellin' that!"

Candy smiled. The first reaction of a customer entering was almost always the same—the sensory experience of being in a shop where chocolate was being melted, dipped, and formed into eye-catching molds and deliciously fine truffles, nut clusters, fudge. "What can I do for you ladies today?" she asked.

"We'll just look some," a tall, stern-looking woman replied.

"Let me know if you need help." She returned to her work behind the counter.

It was always the same: same day of the week, same group of ladies from their weekly Bible study commenting the same comments. "Look at these prices—I could go on over to the drugstore and get me five boxes of Russell Stover for one of these one pounders." —or— "I think she puts *al-ko-hol* in these choc-o-lates!" And Candy's favorite of all the Baptist-lady whispered comments: "This stuff's too rich for my blood!"

Today, the tall woman struck up a bit more conversation than usual. "Say, Candy," she said. "Saw you and your husband at church last Sunday. My, oh my, he has slimmed down. He looks right handsome!"

"Seems like you're not feedin' him any of this chocolate," another woman laughed. "How'd he get that way with you workin' in a candy store?"

Candy wanted to state the obvious: that just because she worked in a chocolate shop did not mean they ate chocolate for breakfast, lunch, and dinner. Always courteous and friendly, she replied, "Why thank you, ma'am, I always thought he was just the handsomest man around!" She laughed her soft rippling laugh and continued, "Yes, my Merle has lost more than eighty pounds. You know it's just a lifestyle change. We cook healthy foods, lotsa veggies. We have chocolate now and then. Merle's real active, exercises, takes good care of himself now."

"Wish I could get my Everett to do that," the plump woman said. "Well, Merle Hucken's sure lookin' good these days!"

"Uh, huh," another lady chimed in. "He's handsome, an' he's a hero in good ol' Fruitvale! Good guy you got there, Candy!"

They all turned to leave. "Thanks for comin' in, ladies. See you next week," Candy said.

Candy headed back to the kitchen behind the retail counter. "Too bad we can't charge those ladies for inhaling our yummy chocolate aroma," she said to Katie Bonnedice, owner of the enterprise.

Katie, preparing to dip amaretto truffles into luscious silky milk chocolate, laughed out loud. "Charge per whiff and a small fee for 'jes' lookin!'"

"That's all the ladies want, after all—is to enjoy the chocolate surroundings and NOT buy a thing!"

Katie slipped the bib of a white apron over her head, tied the ties around her waist. "Oh well, we have lots of good dedicated customers. Who knows? Those ladies might break down and actually buy something one of these days!" She checked the temperature gauge on the tempering machine. "Merle rested up from fighting that awful fire at the judge's house?"

"You know how Merle is; he just keeps going. We feel so bad for the judge and his nice wife. Awful to lose your home."

"They're saying it might be arson. Terrible."

"Merle says they'll catch the bad guys."

Katie laughed. "And Merle Hucken knows something about catching bad guys!" Katie turned to her work. "Thanks for getting the tempering machine up and running. Looks like it's ready to roll."

The stainless-steel tempering machine, humming quietly, melted and brought chocolate to the exact temperature needed for molding chocolate novelties and for coating truffles and nut clusters. Candy had placed thick chunks of chocolate on one side of a baffle that ran through the center of the large stainless-steel bowl. The warming bowl rotated slowly, turning the chunk chocolate into a silky, shiny liquid which pooled out into the opposite side of the baffle.

Katie pulled perfectly round truffle centers from the refrigerator. "Those look great!" She checked the temp again. "Perfect." She methodically dropped the centers, one at a time, into the melted chocolate—pulling them out within two fingers and tapping the excess on the bowl's rim. She transferred the perfectly-coated truffle to a parchment-lined tray, gave a little wrist-twist, and a swirl appeared on the truffle's top.

"Beautiful," Candy said as she observed Katie's technique, "a little work of art!"

"You can do that next batch, Candy—then we'll do nut clusters."

Candy had never been happier. She worked hard in the store, had learned many of the kitchen skills: molding, dipping candy, wrapping and displaying chocolates. She'd grown confident working up front and handling sales. At the end of the workday—tired, but "good tired" as she called it—she'd head home to Maddy and Merle. She felt blessed to have a fun job, a great husband, and a beautiful little girl. If that were not enough, her mother Viv was there with dinner ready and with two-year old Maddy well cared for.

The January day drew to a close; Candy and Katie closed up shop and headed home. Candy arrived at the doublewide, the interior of the home warm and inviting. "Oh, feels good, smells good in here," she said as she shed her coat and gloves. Viv had vegetable soup simmering on the stove and chicken pot pies baking in the oven. She was slicing apples and pears for dessert. Candy gave her mom a kiss on the cheek and picked up Baby Maddy from the floor where she played with her toys. "How's my baby girl? You and Granny Viv have a good day? Daddy home from work?"

Viv answered, "Out for a run, darlin', back in a couple minutes."

Merle blasted in, pushing the door closed behind him. He bent over and held his knees to catch his breath. "Wow, chilly out there," he breathed out. "Hey, how's my pretty lady?" he said.

"Good," Candy answered with a kiss. "Made lots of hearts and fun things for Valentine's Day."

"That's good, sweetie." Merle threw off a jacket and knitted cap and took Maddy from Candy's arms. He placed her on his left forearm and began lifting the twenty-pound toddler like a barbell. Baby Madison Hucken laughed and giggled. Merle counted one, two… completing twenty lifts of the gleeful, giggling toddler. He transferred her to his right forearm. Maddy squealed, "More, dada! More, dada!" Viv and Candy laughed along with Maddy and her father's exercise routine.

Later, they sat down to Viv's home-cooked dinner. After a blessing, Merle said, "Seth got himself quite a surprise today."

"What's that?" Candy asked.

"Got a call from Soon Ha." Merle waited for Viv and Candy's reaction.

"Soon Ha? Is she back? Tell us more!" Both women were wide-eyed with questions.

"All I know is she's back, and Seth's meeting her this evening to talk, so stay tuned."

"Wow, that really is news. Seth must be over the moon."

"Seems so, but I told him to be careful, make sure all's up and legit with her. Reminded him of the fact that her brothers are really bad guys. But, I'll know more tomorrow after Seth's seen her and they've talked."

"Well, in other news," Viv said, "heard me some pret-ty good news today."

"What's that, Granny Viv," Merle asked slurping a spoonful of soup.

"Said on the noon news that Calvin Medernicky was transferred to a mental facility. Judge Stebbins ruled he's a danger to others and to himself, and he's not to be released."

Candy put down her spoon. "That's a great relief, Mama."

"Yes, they showed him being ushered out of the courtroom with handcuffs on his wrists and ankles."

"Couldn't happen to a nicer guy," Merle said sternly.

Viv scooped a spoonful of soup and added, "I wished I coulda asked him how he liked having his hands and feet tied up like that."

CHAPTER 41

THE NEXT MORNING, ANOTHER GRAY January day, Merle and Seth donned their warmest work clothes and set out from the equipment garage. They unloaded chain saws and pruning tools along the highway about 25 miles outside of Fruitvale and quickly discovered one chain saw was not going to start no matter how much they encouraged it. "These darned ol' pieces of junk," Seth complained. "Need this confound tool to clean up those branches whacked down by last week's ice storm. Guess it just don't wanna start on cold winter days."

"Neither do I," Merle chuckled.

"Do what now?"

"Start on cold winter days," Merle said, stifling his heh-hee-heh.

Seth pulled his knit cap closer around his ears. "Merle Hucken, think you oughta know there's a couple hundred thousand comedians outta work so don't plan on bein' one."

Merle emitted another heh-hee-heh and returned to checking the equipment. "Enough already, good buddy. When you gonna tell me about meeting Soon Ha last night?"

"Tell you at lunch, long story," Seth replied.

"Tell you what, Seth-er, we're on company time, but let's open a thermos of coffee and talk about this. Warm up some. Temp out here's 'bout the same as my shoe size."

The two climbed into the cab of the truck. Merle opened the

thermos and poured Seth a cup. "Okay, start from the top, take your time, we'll get all that trimmin' work done… gimme the scoop."

Seth blew steam from the cup and took a sip. A dreamy smile formed on his lips. "She's as pretty as ever, her sweet dimples when she's smiling…"

"Wow, Seth-er, you're kinda hopeless, you know. Clear you're still gone over this gal," Merle said. "But gimme the facts! How's it that she's back, what's goin' on at the barbecue place? That's where she called from, right?"

Seth launched into the details as he heard them from Soon Ha Kim, the woman whom he long considered the love of his life and was convinced he'd lost forever. Now that she was back in his life, it was as if he was renewed, happy, content once again.

"The people who took over the barbecue joint fixed it so Soon Ha and her mother could come back and help in the kitchen. They needed Soon Ha's mom's recipe for kimchi and some of the other special dishes they make. So, they contacted them—through the grapevine, I guess, that they have in Koreatown in Los Angeles. So anyway, they paid their expenses to come back and help them, work again in the restaurant. Like I said, they wanted Soon Ha's mom's style of cooking and experience."

"Who are these people—the ones who took over the place?" Merle asked, a concerned look on his face.

"Koreans from L.A., I guess. They changed the name of the place to "Real Good Barbecue" which is what Soon Ha said is the translation of the old Korean name, Joh Eun BBQ." Seth was quiet and knew Merle would want to know more.

And Merle had more questions. "So, are these people friends, cousins, whoever of Soon Ha? Are they the same family?"

"No, they're not related… though one of Soon Ha's cousins moved back too. He does the book work, an accountant, I think.

And from what Soon Ha said, they're all legal now, got work visas, permits. So, all's good."

"Soon Ha's legal now… she has a valid work permit, no chance she'll be deported. You sure about this?"

"Merle, I believe what she tells me—that her papers are all in order. In a few years, she can maybe apply to become a citizen. She tells me she wants to live here." He smiled, his eyes taking on a dreaminess. "She tells me she wants to live here… with me." He smiled, his sensitive gray eyes looking at the sky.

Merle took this all in. "Well, Seth-er, that's good enough for me. I just want to know that you're not gonna get hurt again, that Soon Ha will not be sent back. Don't think the two of us could handle that!"

Seth smiled and nodded in agreement. "I know she'll be here with me… forever," he said softly.

Finally, Merle asked. "So, what're you gonna do now, Seth-er? How do you feel about what all happened before, I mean, knowin' that Soon Ha's brothers are really, really terrible people." Merle hesitated to say the words, but breathed out, "Killers, drug dealers, really mean and dishonest… guys who did unspeakable things." Merle hoped his words would shake Seth from his dream world, get him to think about what he was reinserting himself into.

The dreamy expression on Seth's handsome face disappeared. "Dunno. Gotta think, Merle." He downed the last of his coffee. "I know that Soon Ha is innocent of all that, that she didn't know what the brothers were up to, that she was hurt as much I was. And one thing's for darn sure, I still love Soon Ha Kim, and I want to marry her." He looked over at Merle and spoke directly. "I'm thinkin' I'm gonna propose to Soon Ha. I want to marry her and marry her soon."

Merle, reflecting on Seth's pronouncement, said nothing. He wondered if he should worry if Seth's heart would be broken for a second time. *Don't think my old pal can take another disappointment like when Soon Ha disappeared.*

Seth broke the silence. "So, you thinkin' about what the boss told you this morning—back at the office?"

"About what?"

"Come on now, Merle, you know what. 'Bout the management part. He offered you a management job."

"Would mean an indoor job. Not out here in the air and all. Seth-er, we've talked about it—how we'd rather be outdoors doin' this than anything else. Would mean managing people—don't know if that's what I do so good."

"Bein' indoors on a day like today would be good, though," Seth said, pulling his cap down around his ears. "Think I'd rather moan about how hot it is in July than put up with this." He pulled on his gloves and opened the door. "Dang, it's cold…"

Merle opened the truck door and climbed out. "Just how cold is it, Seth-er?" he said, speaking over the top of the truck cab.

"It's soooo cold," Seth replied, "that we need ice scrapers for our eyeglasses. How cold is it for you, Merle?"

Merle, chuckling his hee-heh-hee, said, "It's so cold we need electric socks."

The two men headed around the back of the truck and began unloading equipment. Seth, pulling a trimmer from the truck bed, said, "That's nothin!' It's so cold…we got icicles in our coffee thermos."

"That's not very cold. It's so cold at our house, Candy had to open the refrigerator door to warm the house!"

"That's nothing," Seth said. "It's so cold…" He stopped in mid-sentence as a huge truck—a Ford F-550 pickup—black with copious chrome and tinted windows appeared as if out of nowhere. The vehicle screeched to a halt, idling in the highway, right alongside Merle and Seth. Thinking the occupant or occupants might be acquaintances, Merle gave a casual wave and called out, "Hey, there!" Seth strained to see who was in the cab, but the smoky windows made it impossible to glimpse who was driving or who was in the passenger seat.

As quickly as it appeared, the sinister vehicle raced away and disappeared into the cold foggy morning.

"Who was that?" Seth asked.

"You catch the license plate, Seth-er?"

"Nope. Dang."

CHAPTER 42

"**R**EAL NICE OF SETH TO invite us out tonight. Granny Viv's looking after Maddy, nice to be going out for the evening." Candy looked fresh and beautifully groomed. She wore an emerald green sweater and slim jeans. A knitted scarf encircled her neck and reflected colors of her hair and eyes.

Merle held her coat open for her. "Seth wants us to meet Soon Ha. I don't know if you'll like the Korean barbecue. I do."

"You've warned me about the kimchi," Candy said with a laugh.

After the short walk from the car on the chilly night, Merle and Candy entered the restaurant and relished the warmth and savory aromas. Seth rose from a booth and waved to them. He beamed as Merle and Candy joined him. "Soon Ha's back in the kitchen," he said. "Her employer said she could eat dinner with us. Oh, here she is!"

Merle and Candy greeted Soon Ha who bowed slightly to each. She seemed only half Merle's height. He leaned down to smile at her and to shake her hand.

"I so happy meet you, Merle. You Set's very good friend, I know, and I happy meet Miss Candy."

"So nice to meet you, Soon Ha," Candy said. "Are you glad to be back in Fruitvale?"

"Oh, yes, I very happy," Soon Ha replied as they settled into the large booth. Seated with three tall people, she appeared even more petite than ever. She looked directly at Merle, her deep brown eyes shining. "I thank you, Merle, for saving Set from jail. That very bad time, and I worry much about Set. I so sorry for trouble I caused him." Her eyes filled with tears. Seth reached over and held her hand. "It's okay," he said softly.

"I want say, tell you many things so you understand. My mother, I, feel much shame. Very hard us admit wrong, feel shame for brothers. Our culture, very hard admit when family do wrong, make bad mistake. But my mother, we do not know brothers do bad work. We ask forgiveness. My mother she go see Reverend Cho, and we talk him. Other Korean peoples, they say my mother, me, we are bad too, to not talk to us. But Reverend Cho and Mr. Chung, they forgive, help my mother and me find place to stay." Soon Ha brushed away a tear. "I know hard for Mr. Chung. He lost much. Nice lady Marie Chung, she lost much. I very very sad for them. Feel much pain for bad my brothers do." She pulled a tissue from a pocket and cried softly.

Merle, Seth, and Candy were at a loss for words, remained silent as Soon Ha poured out her feelings. "Owners barbecue they help us too. My mother she make kimchi and other Korean foods, and she more happy now."

Soon Ha dried tears. She turned to Seth. "I love you, Set. Thank you let me meet your good friends."

Candy and Merle could not think of a thing to say. Seth, trying to subdue his thumping heart, held her hand and whispered, "Maybe we should order some dinner now."

CHAPTER 43

"**T**HINK THIS NEW CHAIN SAW can handle that icy brush along the trees, Merle?"

"Yep, just be careful… don't drive off into a ditch 'cuz you're thinking about your sweetie, Soon Ha," Merle said. He emitted a muffled hee-heh-hee. He and Seth were bundled against the cold of the wintry day.

"Thinkin' about proposing to the girl, Merle," Seth said, breathing out a foggy cloud.

"Well, that's good 'cept I might say you should take your time, let things settle down some, see how it goes for Soon Ha and her mom."

"Why? I've waited too long already!"

"It's just that her brothers are on death row, and seems to me that kinda thing can really affect a family and all," Merle said thoughtfully.

Seth didn't answer for some time. He inspected the equipment. "It's just that my life has been on hold for too long. I want to be with Soon Ha." He started the engine which promptly sputtered out. "Dad-gum, crappy motor," he complained. "Stupid machine's supposed to mow back the icy branches that are down. Won't if the dang thing won't start."

Merle chuckled. "Maybe we'll get some work done today, Seth-er, if the equipment cooperates." He checked the oil gauge.

"Say, I'm wondering… how it is when a Korean marries a not-Korean? Any special things you gotta remember?"

"Like what?"

"I dunno—maybe there's a tradition on how a guy proposes—or how he asks for the lady's hand in marriage, so to speak."

"Oh, gotcha. I asked Soon Ha's cousin that. He said it's pretty much the same as for Americans 'cept it's good to give the bride's mom a goose."

"Excuse me? What did you just say?" Merle could hardly contain himself. He spun his tall frame in a circle and guffawed. "The bridegroom gives the mother-in-law a goose!" He bent over, held his knees, and howled.

"Oh, for crap's sake, Merle, the bridegroom gives the mother-in-law a live goose, preferably a wild goose he's caught. I guess they cook it later for a special meal—or some such thing." Seth put on his best serious face and waited for Merle to recover.

Merle choked out words. "That's not what I thought you said!" He stood up and held his sides. He bent over again as he began howling with laughter again. "Can just see you catchin' a live goose and bringin' it to Soon Ha's mom!" Merle could not control his merriment. "I can just see you carryin' a goose—how do you do that? Grab it by its legs and carry it upside down?" He held his sides. "And jes' for the record, good buddy, do not ask me to go on a 'wild goose chase' to help you!" He placed his hands on the mower seat, bent over, and laughed and laughed. "Jeez, you're makin' me cry. Tears gonna freeze on my cheeks out here in this cold weather!"

"Oh, for cryin' out loud, Merle, give it up, would ya?" Seth elbowed Merle from the mower seat. "Outta my way, Hucken, somebody's gotta get some work done today." Merle, wiping tears of laughter from his face with the backs of his gloved hands, recovered and began assisting Seth. They tested the mower's distributor and assessed the mechanical problem. As the two men worked alongside one another, they sensed noise and motion approaching on the deserted highway. They both straightened and looked to their right and down the highway.

Again, materializing out of nowhere as if in a horror movie, the huge black Ford pickup with four doors and six tires raced up alongside Seth and Merle. The driver hit the brakes, and the big vehicle idled alongside the two startled men. Seth and Merle strained to see who was in the truck, but the dark windows were completely opaque.

"Hello?" Merle called out. "What you guys need? Hey, there! Something we can do for you?"

No response from the driver or the passenger, if there was one in the pickup. Suddenly, the driver gunned the motor, and the mystery vehicle sped away, disappearing in a trail of exhaust. The highway was once again deserted.

"Who are those guys?" Seth asked. "An' what the heck do they want?"

CHAPTER 44

T HE FOYER LEADING TO THE district attorney's office was shoulder-to-shoulder with news personnel juggling cameras and microphones. Tanequa Milwood, slim, well-dressed, and poised as always, entered and began, "Thank you for coming this morning. I'd like to announce the sentencing of Delbert Judd, former sheriff of Fremont County. You'll recall Mr. Judd was accused of aiding and abetting illegal drug trafficking and of accepting payment for his helping the Kim brothers to conduct their illegal activities. In addition, he was charged as an accessory to the murder of Jimmy Chung, a local businessman. And you'll recall the jury found Delbert Judd guilty on all counts. At his sentencing hearing today, he was sentenced to 29 years in prison without possibility of parole. He will be transferred to Central Prison.

"How'd he take the news, Ms. Milwood?" a television reporter called out.

"As well as anyone who's guilty as charged," responded the D.A.

"Any chance for parole?" another questioned.

"I believe I said Delbert Judd will never be paroled."

That night, Tanequa Milwood's car veered from the highway and hit a massive oak tree straight on. She sustained serious injuries.

CHAPTER 45

KATIE BONNEDICE—WEARING A BRIGHT-WHITE APRON, her dark hair pulled back from her pretty face—looked up from perusing a register print-out. The pre-Valentine sales had been brisk, and she was checking the day's sales.

"Afternoon, gentlemen," she said as two men entered. They did not respond, but looked around as if they had a purpose in mind. "Help you find something?" Katie asked.

"Nope," the younger of the two men snapped. In his mid-forties, his short stature carried a slight paunch; his thinning hair was combed straight back. The other man, older but with a similar build, wore a black ball cap with "WVA" in block lettering. The two men and their similarity of stature would bring one to believe they could be brothers—or at least related.

"Let me know if I can help," Katie said. "Please feel free to browse."

"We're gonna do jes' that, ma'am," the older of the two said. Their demeanor was chilly, unfriendly at best.

The men, both wearing jeans, work boots, and heavy jackets, strode around looking at merchandise. Neither commented, but—at one time or another—both peered into the kitchen where Candy was cleaning the fudge machine. "That lady there—she work here all the time?" one man asked.

"Yes, she's a full-timer, sir," Katie replied. The men were making her uneasy, but she remained pleasant. "You know, we make all our chocolates here in our kitchen—molded novelties, fudge, truffles."

"That so," the younger said. He turned his back to Katie and shoved his gloved hands in the pockets of his jacket. "Les' go, Donny, seen enough." He headed to the door; the other followed. The shop door slammed behind them; the tinkling door bells shuddered.

Katie, looking concerned, returned to the kitchen. "Candy, those were two odd birds who were just in… if I didn't know better, I'd think they were casing the joint."

"Maybe they're competition?" Candy asked. "Getting ready to open a chocolate shop?"

"Somehow, don't think they're the chocolate shop type. Rough around the edges. Kinda unnerved me." Katie's big brown eyes looked worried. "Well, if they think they're going to rob us someday, they're not going to get big money from my candy store! They'd do better just robbing a bank!"

The bells on the store door jingled again. Marie Chung entered and closed the door quietly.

"Marie!" Candy called from the kitchen. "Come on back here! Wonderful to see you!"

Marie, wearing a charcoal coat with a thick pale gray pashmina wrapped to withstand the winter chill, came into the kitchen. Her generally serene face reflected worry and concern. "Oh my, Candy, did you hear the awful news?"

Candy's heart sank. "Oh, no, what now?"

"Tanequa Milwood was in an awful accident. She's in the hospital. Hurt real, real bad."

At home that evening, Candy and Merle made plans to visit Tanequa in the hospital. "I put together a basket with chocolate and treats. Maybe it'll cheer her, I hope," Candy said.

"I dunno, sweetie," Merle said, his clear blue eyes narrowing. "The DA just drove right off the road and hit a giant oak tree. Airbag saved her, but she's still hurt bad."

"She's such a hard worker," Candy replied. "She must have been very tired, maybe fell asleep at the wheel?"

"I dunno. Bad things happen to good people, dunno why." Merle sat, lost in thought. "Sorry, sweetie, didn't ask about your day, pretty lady."

"Busy… people buying valentine gifts. We did have two strangers come in, who just acted kinda peculiar."

"Whadya mean peculiar?"

"As if they were 'casing the joint,' as Katie put it. They were looking around, peeking into the kitchen. Didn't seem they were interested in the merchandise, just that they were looking for something else."

Merle thought for a moment. "Were they driving a big ol' Ford pickup with fancy chrome, big mudflaps, dark windows, and doodads all over? If I'm not mistaken, it has two extra tires on the rear. Six tires! Serious pickup truck?"

"Couldn't see what they were driving. I was back in the kitchen."

Merle placed his napkin on the table and said nothing.

"What're you thinking, Merle, honey?"

"I'm thinkin' there are bad guys in Fruitvale."

With seriously bruised eyes, Tanequa Milwood looked up at her visitors. Merle and Candy entered the hospital room loaded with gifts—a beautiful basket with chocolate goodies and a stack of current magazines for her to read when she felt better. "You two are the best," she said.

Merle took her hand. "How ya doin?"

"Better. Have to have surgery on my knees, but the facial

things should heal okay. Lost a tooth. She managed a weak smile to show the gap in her front teeth.

"I'm so sorry this happened!" Candy said. "Wish I had me a magic wand. I'd wave it and fix you up fine."

"The thought is lovely, Candy. Thanks."

"You recall what happened?" Merle asked.

Tanequa moved her shoulder, grimaced with pain. "Reason to believe," she said slowly, "the brakes on my car were tampered with."

"What?" Merle asked incredulously.

"My car is pretty new, passed the safety inspection just days ago. Investigator checked the brakes; fluid line was cut. When I braked at a stop sign and started to make a left turn, the car didn't slow, just kept going right into trees across the road. Happened so fast; I hit the brakes but…"

Merle's jaw tightened; his ordinarily cheerful face darkened. "Some weird things goin' on, Ms. Milwood… got me worried."

"Me too, Merle. Rodney Taylor's on it." She shifted gingerly and squeezed Merle's hand. "Merle, when are you going to call me Tanequa? We've been through so much together," she asked.

"Merle smiled and could only say, "Yes, ma'am. I mean—Tanequa!"

On the way home, Candy asked, "Why would anyone want to hurt Tanequa Milwood. She only does what's needed, puts bad people out of business."

"Maybe there are bad people still 'in business' who don't like what she's doing," Merle said, thoughtfully. "Think I'll call Agent Taylor. Gotta a couple things to ask 'im."

CHAPTER 46

THE LATE FEBRUARY MORNING WAS clear but not as cold. Seth and Merle cruised along in the state truck on their way to clean up storm damage on Highway 85. "Not icy, today," Merle said. "Won't be no time an' we'll clean up that mess. Hope there's not too many branches we'll have to saw up."

"Got that new chain saw. Oughta do good," Seth said. The two friends cruised along in silence each lost in his own thoughts.

"Not so cold now—regular heat wave happening," Merle was saying, when without warning and completely surprising, the threatening black pickup appeared and raced up behind. Tailgating, menacing.

"Who are those guys?" Seth asked, a frightened look crossing his face. He glanced back nervously. "And what do they want?"

Suddenly the powerful engine of the pickup roared as the driver pulled up alongside Merle and Seth. Merle released his foot from the gas, slowed; the menacing vehicle kept pace alongside. Suddenly it veered dangerously close. Merle swerved and lurched off the road and applied the brakes. The huge pickup raced on by, its big V-8 motor gunning.

Merle and Seth each sighed relief. "What the heck?" Seth yelled. "What in god's name are they doing, and what in the name of Jehovah do they want?"

Merle did not answer; he dialed Rodney Taylor. "Agent Taylor! That big Ford F-550 I told you about? They're ba-a-a-ck.

Drove Seth and me off the road. We're out here on 85 about 20-some miles outside Mossville… yep… okay, we're headin' back. See you back at the state equipment garage."

Twenty minutes later, Merle and Seth pulled into the state highway division site. Rodney Taylor waited, pacing.

"Hey, Agent Taylor, somebody's tryin' to kill us!" Merle said as he and Seth exited the truck.

"Ya think?" Rodney Taylor said, his eyes hard and angry. "SBI's fully on this, plus we asked for a team of U.S. Marshals here to protect you, Seth, Tanequa, and Judge Stebbins."

"What about you?" Merle asked.

"Yeah, me too. Someone shot at my house during the night."

"Family okay?" Merle's heart pounded. "I hate this bad stuff."

"Everyone's okay, Merle. Like I said, U.S. Marshals are here—they're watching your house too."

Merle sighed a small measure of relief. "Still need to find who these guys are."

"My concern it has to do with the Korean mafia. Mafia spreads far and wide. Since you and Tanequa and I helped bring down the local group—indirectly—they're exacting revenge."

Merle spoke slowly, "We know a couple of things: can't be Delbert Judd; he's in prison—along with the Kim brothers. Can't be Calvin Medernicky: he's in restraints in a mental hospital, and he's got no one to go to bat for him."

"And," Rodney Taylor added, "his cousin Willy Lawson will be sentenced soon for tampering with evidence and for taking a bribe to do so. Nobody's gonna help him either."

"So, who're these guys in the big fancy truck who's runnin' us off the road and hangin' around the chocolate shop? Candy's boss was freaked out by them."

"SBI's close to identifying those guys in the Ford F-550. Agency's putting together a plan, ready in about 24 hours. If you're needed to help, Merle, you okay with that? How 'bout you, Seth?"

"You betcha, Agent Taylor," Merle said.

"Let's get the bad guys off the road," Seth added, nodding in agreement.

"Yep, tell us what you need us to do," Merle said, his arms folded across his wide chest. "Gotta get Fruitvale back to the nice quiet and safe town it used to be."

That night, Merle did not tell Candy about the day's terrifying events nor did he mention he and Seth had agreed to help Agent Taylor and the SBI. *Not gonna worry Candy 'bout this. Woulda thought by now all this grief'd be behind us— that we'd all be safe and live our lives good and not worry so much. Hope this is the last time Seth-er and I have to deal with bad guys.*

CHAPTER 47

THE NEXT MORNING, CANDY ARRIVED at the back door
of the chocolate shop. As she pulled the door key from her
handbag, a wintry breeze floated the door open. *Oh, Katie's here.
Guess she didn't close the door tight.*

Candy entered, but the kitchen was dark. She flipped on
lights. *This is odd.* "Katie? You here?" she called out at she
stowed her purse and coat.

Candy glanced across the kitchen and past the wrapping
counter. She caught sight of something slumped over the tempering machine. Feeling faint, she grabbed the nearby counter and
held on. "Oh, my lord! No! No!"

Candy, her heart racing and her mind spinning, recognized
the body of Katie Bonnedice, her face submerged in now solidi-
fied chocolate, her body draped over and supported on a stack of
fifty-pound boxes of semi-sweet chocolate. A piece of cardboard
wedged in between her left arm and her lifeless body read: "How
do you like your Candy now?"

Weeping and hysterical, Candy called for help.

The chocolate shop sign was turned to "Closed," but the small
shop was far from empty. Law enforcement filled the small shop

and kitchen. A forensics team and photographers jostled to do their work. An ambulance had come and departed carrying Katie Bonnedice's body.

Candy, weeping, sat on a stool behind the fudge counter. A policewoman placed an arm around Candy's shoulders when she seemed ready to collapse. Rodney Taylor spoke softly, "Candy, this is hard, but tell me everything you saw when you entered the kitchen this morning."

"Horrible," Candy sputtered out, wadding a tissue between fingertips, "finding Katie like that. For a moment, I couldn't recognize who, what —then I saw her red Crocs she wore a lot, her striped chef's pants. They had her folded over, sort of hanging over boxes of bulk chocolate with her face…" Candy pushed a lock of hair from her forehead then drifted to the right. The policewoman caught her before she fell from the stool.

The shop door sounded its tinkling entry, and Merle Hucken strode into the space. "Sweetie! They called me at work—what happened? Rod—what's goin' on?"

An SBI agent tapped Rodney Taylor on the shoulder. "Sorry to interrupt, sir, but you need to see this."

Rodney Taylor returned to the kitchen. The agent pointed to a large box of bulk chocolate with writing scrawled on the side. It read: "Merle, you're next."

At home, Candy fell into bed and pulled the covers tight around her. Merle sat at her side and stroked her hair. "Sweetie, you've been through a terrible thing. Granny Viv and I are here for you. We'll get through this, my pretty lady. The police and SBI will find who did this awful thing."

Candy sobbed as if the end of the world had arrived. "They thought they were killing me! They're going to kill you!"

Merle said nothing. He laid his head on her shivering shoulder. "We're gonna get these bad guys. I'm making you a promise, my beautiful wife. We're gonna get those guys."

Merle tucked covers around Candy and stood. "Try to rest, sweetie."

Granny Viv held Maddy who seemed confused by her mother's tearful arrival and departure straight to the bedroom. Viv asked, "Merle, what happens now? What are the SBI and Rodney Taylor going to do now?"

"They're puttin' a plan in place to get those guys. Pretty sure it's the two yahoos who are racin' around in that big Ford pickup." Merle took Maddy from Viv's arms and held her close. The toddler tipped her curly blonde head and rested it on Merle's broad shoulder. "US Marshals are here to protect the district attorney, Judge Stebbins, and… us. Don't worry Viv. In a day or so, those guys'll be behind bars. I guar-an-tee it."

Viv walked to the front window and lifted the shade. Two U.S. marshals stood watch.

"You guarantee they'll get those bad guys? As long as you're not part of the 'getting,' Merle," Viv said softly, her face reflecting fear and concern.

"Don't you worry, Granny Viv, all this will be healed in time. Please don't worry."

CHAPTER 48

MERLE AND SETH SET OUT to drive along Highway 201-37, a quiet two-lane stretch north of Fruitvale. "Agent Taylor said to just cruise and see if the guys show up. SBI and sheriff's deputies are in the area if something starts to happen."

Seth, nervous and uncomfortable in the passenger side of the big state truck, tugged at a Kevlar vest. "This thing's chokin' me. Think the vest'll kill me before a bullet does," he complained.

"Loosen up the Velcro straps at the shoulders," Merle instructed. "Yank it down some, more comfortable that way. Good you're not a fatty, Seth-er. When I last wore this contraption, my belly was lots bigger, an' it itched and rubbed. Fits better when you're not so fat."

"So, what do we do when the guys in the devil truck show up?" Seth asked as he fiddled with the vest's straps.

"No worries, Seth-er. Police helicopter's trackin' us. Those two devils try something, the SBI team'll come an' get 'em."

"Cold comfort," Seth said quietly. His generally smooth brow was furled, his chiseled jaw set.

"Say what? I have no idea what that means, Seth-er." Merle glanced up at the rear-view mirror. "Uh, oh," he said quietly. "Trouble."

Seth craned his neck around. "Yep, devils! Careful, Merle! They're gonna tailgate us!"

"Yep, they're on our tail. Stay cool, Seth-er."

The big pickup followed dangerously close, its high hood even with the flatbed, its shiny chrome front bumper tapping the rear of the state truck. Merle slowed; the pickup kept pace. Occasionally the pickup driver would gun the motor as if he'd put the transmission in neutral and hit the gas pedal. The sound of the powerful engine was loud and threatening.

"This is crazy," Seth breathed out. "What are they doing? What'll we do when they try to run us off the road again?"

Without warning, the big vehicle sped up and pulled around in front of Merle and Seth, then immediately slowed. The license plate was easy to read. Seth asked, "West Virginia? Who's from over there an' wants to kill us?"

Merle tapped the brakes to keep from slamming into the high rear bumper of the Ford. Seth grabbed at the dashboard as the state truck rocked forward. As the "devil truck" cruised at a slow speed, Merle attempted to drop further behind.

A motorist, braking to slow well below the posted speed limit, pulled up behind Merle and Seth. Merle lowered the window and waved the car around. The motorist sped around Merle and the big pickup up ahead. "I'm pulling over," Merle said. "See what they do."

"Where's this SBI team you keep promising me, Merle?" Seth was agitated; his hands shook.

Merle didn't answer as he turned the truck from the highway and on to the shoulder. The pickup gleamed in the winter morning sunshine and sped ahead. Traffic had piled up behind.

"Wow," Seth said, fidgeting and perspiring. "Weird. Who are those guys? Are they mafia guys? Is there Korean mafia in West Virginia?"

When the traffic passed and the road cleared, Merle pulled back onto the highway. "Well, they're gone now. At least we saw the West Virginia plate. You get the number, Seth-er?"

"Naw, got too nervous when I saw that big freakin' truck."

"Okay, we know it's a Ford F-550 6X6 from West Virginia. Rodney Taylor and his team'll find out…"

Suddenly, the huge menacing vehicle reappeared, this time approaching from the left lane. It slowed alongside, then made a sudden U-turn, again pulling in behind Merle and Seth. Merle tried to concentrate on driving, struggled to remain composed and to keep the truck under control. The pickup followed too close. As soon as traffic in the left lane cleared, the black pickup again yanked crazily to the left and pulled up alongside Merle and Seth. Merle stayed steady, driving straight ahead. "Agent Taylor said the police helicopter'll track," he muttered.

"And just where's all those police and helicopters they said'll be here to help us?" Seth was yelling.

"Stay cool, Seth-er… gonna be okay." Merle kept the state truck at an even speed. The black truck again dropped behind as left lane traffic approached.

Seth, his neck and shoulders craning, turned to stare out the back windshield. "Ye-gods, Merle! The devil truck's gotta a moon roof! Guy's standin' up in it —- and Merle! He's gotta rifle!"

From the truck's rear-view mirror, Merle caught sight of the barrel of a rifle. He calmly began swerving the truck— left to right and back again—then straight ahead—then right to left. Seth unsnapped his seat belt and turned his lean body to watch, his hands gripping the back of the seat. "He's aimin', Merle! He's aimin' at us!"

Merle gunned the motor of the state truck and raced ahead, but again the black pickup kept pace directly behind with the gunman balancing himself and aiming from the moon roof.

Two shots rang out. The back windshield of the state truck shattered, and a fraction of a second later the front windshield crazed with piercing of bullets. Merle struggled to control the truck; at last he yanked the swerving vehicle off the road and onto the shoulder. The truck tipped crazily as Merle braked to stop. Seth was thrown forward but held on.

As the Ford F-550 raced on ahead, the whirr of helicopter blades was music to Merle's ears. The sound grew loud and rumbling as the helicopter settled to land on the highway. Merle lowered the driver side window and looked out and up; it was impossible to see through the crazed windshield. Fragments fell forward into his lap.

"Wow, that was close, Seth-er!" Merle removed his cap and willed his pounding heart to calm. "By now, the roadblock ahead's probably got the devils and their fancy truck." He flicked a shard of windshield glass from his lap and replaced his cap. The windstorm of the spinning helicopter blades calmed him; the truck sat at a slant and vibrated. He exhaled and looked over at his friend Seth.

Seth slumped toward him and moaned softly. He held the side of his head; blood flowed through his fingers.

"Seth-er! Seth-er!"

At a distance, sirens wailed. Gunfire cracked.

At the hospital, Seth underwent surgery to repair a head wound. "Bullet grazed the side of his head, just above the ear. He's healthy," the surgeon pronounced, "and he'll heal quickly."

"Can I see him now?" Merle asked, his usually ruddy color drained from his face.

"He's coming out of the anesthetic. Give him a couple of hours."

CHAPTER 49

A week later, Merle and Seth were invited to Tanequa Milwood's office. She wanted to share further results of the intensive investigation into the two men from West Virginia.

As Merle and Seth entered the foyer of the D.A.'s office, they heard, "Hey, Merle. Hey, Seth." They spun around to greet SBI Agent Rodney Taylor. The three entered the D.A.'s office together. Each leaned down to hug Tanequa Milwood who was seated in a wheelchair. She was thinner, but looked remarkably well considering her serious injuries from the car crash. Recently back at work, she appeared upbeat and happy. She smiled and said, "How are the three bravest men in this entire state?"

"More important," Merle said, "how's the bravest lady of all?"

"I'm not sure who that is," she laughed, "but I'll accept it as a compliment. I'm doing good. Lots of physical therapy. Walking better each day. They hired a full-time assistant for me, so I'm not so slammed with work these days. It's all good!"

"So, Tanequa, let's bring Merle and Seth up to date on the drivers of the "devil truck"—as Seth calls it." Rodney Taylor laughed and turned to Seth. "How's that bullet line you added to your haircut?"

"Healing," Seth replied. "Had a major headache early on, but fine now. Told my mom that being in jail when I wasn't guilty was a worse experience. Thanks to you all, I got outta that one!"

"So good you're doing well, Seth. Took a lot of courage to ride along with Merle that day we arrested the guys from West Virginia."

"Yep," Merle added, "Seth insisted on it. Said if I was gonna wear a bullet-proof vest, he wanted one too." Merle stifled a hee-hey-hee.

"And Merle, I need to know how Candy's doing. She went through a terrible trauma. She better?" Tanequa asked. "Not fair to have to find a victim… terrible…"

Merle sighed. "I was so worried she'd slip back in a depression, but she's seeing a counselor; and Marie Chung—bless her—has been a great friend to Candy. Helps her a lot." Merle twisted his cap in his hands. "Candy's doing better but misses Katie and her job. She's taking a computer class, spending more time with Maddy and Viv, keeps busy. I'm proud she's overcome so much. Katie Bonnedice's family… Katie was the owner of the chocolate shop, you recall… anyway, they're thinking about reopening, relocating the business. They asked if Candy would consider helping 'em run the business. Candy said she wasn't ready to make a decision yet, but that she'd think on it."

"Understandable, considering how traumatic… but maybe when she's recovered some, it might be a good opportunity for Candy." Tanequa was silent for a moment. "Well, let me get to some real good news: as you know, the drivers of the "devil truck" are behind bars and awaiting trial. We threw the book at them: murder of Katie Bonnedice, attempted murder—you'll recall they disabled the brakes on my car, and need I remind you they tried to run you guys off the road. Oh, and let's add arson, threatening, creating mayhem… the list goes on and on."

"So, who are those guys? Mafia from West Virginia?"

"Hardly," Rodney Taylor interjected. "Brothers. Last name's Judd."

No one spoke for moments. Seth, wide-eyed, yelled out, "Judd? As in Sheriff Delbert Judd?"

"None other," Tanequa replied. "Delbert Judd's brothers Donny and Dean. When they sat through Delbert Judd's trial, the assistant D.A. watched them a lot. One day, he said to me, out of the blue, 'I think those guys are psychotic.' Boy, he called that right."

"Seemed they were holed up in a bed and breakfast out at Wexsapahaw," Rodney Taylor added. "The owner of the B&B was concerned, thought they were up to something nefarious, but there was nothing specific she felt she should report. When she found out they murdered Katie Bonnedice, she was really upset. Lots of regrets."

"Well, we're going to trial with tons of evidence again them, so hopefully all the Judd brothers will spend the rest of their days in prison," Tanequa added.

"Couldn't happen to nicer guys," Merle said. He looked relieved; the color had returned to his face. "At least the bad guys are off the road once and for all." He bent his tall frame down to hug Tanequa. "You take care now, Miss Tanequa. Don't work so hard. Let that helper of yours take on some of the load." Merle extended his hand to Rodney Taylor. "And thanks for sending people to protect my family and me."

Rodney replied, "You were instrumental in getting those guys, Merle."

"And for getting me outta jail for something I didn't do," Seth said, patting his old friend on the back.

Merle blushed a ruddy rose. "Uh, ya'll… we need to get back to work. Thanks for tellin' us what's what with the bad guys. It's a great to know Fruitvale's a safer place now." He placed his cap on his head and said, "Seth-er, let's go mow."

"You got it, Merle."

ACKNOWLEDGEMENTS

Without the patience and encouragement of Steve, Lyn, and Antonia Kristen, this novel would not have happened. Thank you, my beautiful family, for all you do for me!

To my beta readers: Thank you to Jean Earnhardt, Linda Birkhead, and Stephanie Moore for your wisdom and thoughtful critiques. Your friendship means the world to me!

To Glendon at Streetlight Graphics and to Sandra Arizmendi: Thank you for translating my whacky ideas into professional images. I am so grateful for your caring help and expertise.

And thank you to all the Merles out there—the really good guys (and gals)—who know right from wrong, work hard, and take care of their families and communities.

ABOUT THE AUTHOR

Katherine Fuoco Fairchild has always been interested in relationships: how siblings and family interact, how friendships develop and how they strengthen, how colleagues relate to one other. She translates that interest into essays, short stories, and novels.

She has taught middle-school English and English as a second language and has worked in and established retail businesses.

She and her husband have lived in five states and in Belgium, Hong Kong, Singapore, and Australia.

Presently, she and SJ Fairchild live and write in North Carolina.

Instagram: Katherine_Fuoco_Fairchild
Twitter: @fairfuoco
Website: fairfuoco.com